SARA:
A PRINCESS IN THE MAKING
The Journey Begins

CHERYL OLSON

This book was edited by Lisa Thompson. You can email her at writebylisa@gmail.com or visit her website at www.writebylisa.com.
Cover design and print format by Alice Briggs at www.kingdomcovers.com.
Artist: Isaiah Batten

Disclaimer: This book contains sensitive and adult subject matter that could upset some readers.

ISBN: 978-0-9988435-2-0
Published by
Cheryl Olson/Eagle's Garden
P.O. Box 4162
Brookings Oregon 97415

Dedicated it to my loving husband Daniel D. Olson who
has supported me from the time we said "I do" thirty
years ago

SARA:
A PRINCESS
IN THE MAKING

INTRODUCTION

The five-year-old girl played on the swing, her fine blonde curls trailing behind her as she rocked back and forth. The sturdy swing hung from an oak tree, it's bark rough in spots. . She watched as the man walked from the front yard leaving the side gate open as he walked up to her. He was in his mid-twenties, clean-shaven, with very curly hair and bright blue eyes. His left hand was hidden in his leather jacket. Not in a pocket, but inside the jacket itself. Sara thought his eyes looked kind, but he still scared her for some reason that she couldn't put her finger on.

"Hi, Sara! My name is Mike. Your mommy is very sick, so she asked me to take you to stay with me tonight. I'll bring you back home in the morning."

"But Gamma will be home soon. I can wait for her, and she will take care of Mommy. Thank you, anyway." Sara continued to swing, kicking her slender legs to gain momentum. She wished this man would just go away.

Mike was persistent as he continued. "Do you like to play Chicken?"

As soon as Sara heard the secret word, she smiled.

"Chicken is the secret word mommy told me." Sara paused and looked up at the stranger again, her green eyes big with wonder. "Okay. I can go with you."

The precocious child hopped off the swing. She took Mike's right hand as he offered it, grasping it with her left hand. Together, the pair walked from the back yard through the tall grass to the driveway in the front of the house. The paper crown resting on her head floated to the ground behind her. Sara took no notice as she concentrated on the man's hand and worried about her sick mother.

He situated her in the nondescript white van sitting in front of the house. While it was certainly not Mike's car of choice, it took him and his cargo where they needed to go. She relaxed as Mike buckled her into the car seat in the back row. He got into the driver's seat and put in a lullaby CD. Within seconds, he started the car, and the powerful engine roared to life. Looking both ways, he backed out of the driveway.

Sara looked at her house over her shoulder, watching as it grew smaller and smaller in the distance.

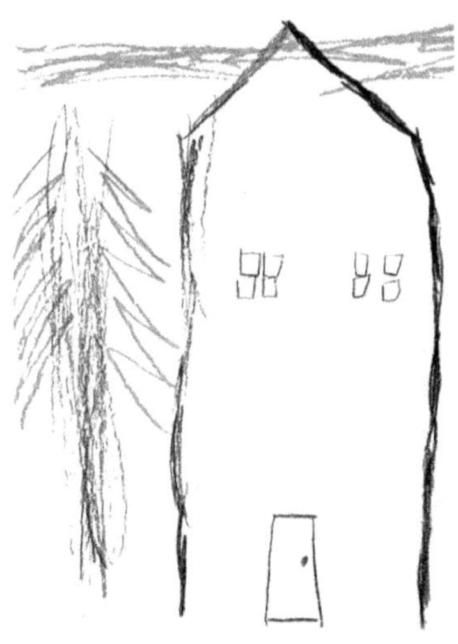

CHAPTER 1

"Christine! I'm home," the older woman called out as she carried two bags of groceries through the kitchen door from the garage. "Sara, honey, Gamma's got a treat for you!" Paula set the groceries down on the counter. The house seemed too quiet with a child as active as Sara.. Paula sensed that something was wrong before she even walked through the kitchen into the living room where her daughter lay passed out on the couch.

"Christine! Wake up! Where is Sara?" She pushed at Christine's body in an attempt to rouse her from her doped-up slumber.
Christine coughed, groaned, and rolled over to face the couch. "Leave me alone."

"You are not answering my question. Where is my granddaughter?"

"It's all your fault! If you hadn't hid your valuables or if you'd given me money, I wouldn't have had to sell her!" Christine turned, sat up, and glared at her mother. The glazed look in Christine's eyes told Paula everything she needed to know. The needle and the rubber tubing she used as a tourniquet were carelessly tossed on the floor, confirming Paula's worst fears.

"Christine! What have you done with your daughter?" Paula's eyes welled up with tears. Her stomach knotted up with tension, and she grew lightheaded at the thought of what had happened to her granddaughter.

"She will be home in the morning," Christine replied. "Take your disappointment in me somewhere else."

Paula backed away,, glaring at Christine. She raced around the house, still struggling to believe that Sara was really gone. After a thorough search convinced her that the child was not inside, she ran into the backyard, hoping to find the girl on the swing. When she saw that Sara wasn't there, she called her name again and again.

"Saraaaaaaaaa! Saraaaaaaaaaa!" She stretched out the child's name, praying that her voice would carry the words where her feet would not go.

She stopped short, almost tripping over the paper crown sitting in the grass. Her shoulders slumped in defeat at the sight.

Walking back along the side yard and closing the gate that was left open she started to head inside to call 911. The cut phone wires at the side of the house stuck out like a sore thumb. So much for that idea, she thought.

As she looked across her front yard to the street, her neighbor was watering the lawn. She started toward her friend's home to ask for help.

A voice threatened her from behind. "You aren't going anywhere, Gamma, so you best turn yourself around and go back to the house stay inside for the night."

Paula turned around to find the source of the threat. A large stocky older man dressed in a black suit and striped tie stood in the hedge by her driveway. He carelessly stomped on the rose bush that she had planted in memory of her late husband. She hoped a sharp thorn would scratch his ankle but no such luck. "We need to set some new ground rules around here since my men will be spending time here keeping your daughter supplied with what she needs." He firmly gripped her arm in his, guiding her back to the house, slamming the door shut behind her. She barely had time to glance back across the street at her neighbor. As the door slammed shut, so did a door in her heart. The cold realization slowly dawned on Paula: she was a prisoner in her own home.

Once inside, tears formed in her eyes for the second time within an hour. She looked around her precious home. Together, she and her late husband Brad had painstakingly planted the front garden, watering according to schedule. Brad had painted the front of the house and porch in welcoming colors, white for the exterior and yellow for the framing. Paula loved how cheery it was even on the most overcast of days. She kept the inside clean and dusted even if the furniture was a bit dated. And the back yard was a private haven where a cool breeze refreshed them after the warmest of days. Despite Brad's health issues, he still managed to sweep the front porch and rake a few leaves.

But now, she was trapped inside.

Paula went into the kitchen to put away the unattended groceries, trying to keep busy as she held back the tears. The man in the black suit sat down at the kitchen table next to a window overlooking the back yard. The swing that Sara so loved was swaying back and forth in the breeze. The once-immaculate backyard showed signs of Brad's passing as if the yard itself grieved the absence of its owner. The overgrown grass had some brown spots, half dead from a lack of watering.

"Sit down, Gamma." The thug motioned at her with

his thick right hand, gesturing for her to sit at the kitchen table.

She complied, facing the man before her with contempt in her eyes. He scoffed at her discomfort. He was very overweight with a thick accent that she couldn't quite place. Despite the nicely tailored suit, an air of evil surrounded him. As he spoke, she felt as if the devil himself had invaded her home with no way to remove him. She prayed silently for the Father to help her.

"I admit that you will need to adjust to these new conditions, but I'm sure you will cooperate if you want your daughter and granddaughter to live. Am I correct?" His face remained blank as he spoke. Paula slowly nodded. "Good. That's the first step. Now you will continue with your daily life as long as we are here. That will be as long as your daughter can facilitate our needs, and we will do the same for her.

"You can attend church and its functions, shop, and go to lunch with friends, but we won't ever be far away. You even breathe differently, and your precious family will be gone. Your daughter needs us to keep her habit going, and men need your granddaughter. They will pay me much more than what the drugs your daughter value so much," he said stoically. "So do we have an understanding? We have to protect our interests."

"What you are doing is despicable!" Paula glared at him. "What is happening with Sara? And why are you keeping me as a prisoner in your game?"

"You can leave anytime you want. We can just call it quits right now, but I don't think you want two funerals to deal with this week," the man replied.

Paula slumped back in her chair, defeated. This morning, Sara and Christine were sitting at this very table, chatting and laughing. For a short moment, Paula had thought life would return to normal again. Sara ate everything on her plate and giggled as her mom tickled her and joked with her. She longed for that moment again, which seemed so distant now.

Now strangers had invaded her home of thirty years, the home built with her husband. She knew every nail that they had pounded into the walls. Most days, she thought she could still smell the newly spread plaster over the sheet rock on the walls. Now the pretty pink valances with the decorative rose ties over the kitchen windows failed to brighten the invading darkness. Even the shiny stainless steel sink lost its gleam as if it knew it was shining too brightly and needed to tone down. The cheerful atmosphere crept out of the residence, sensing the change in the house that was so loved.

The man seemed familiar, but she wasn't sure how she knew him. Her lack of memory played to her advantage. "Fine, I'll do it," Paula conceded, putting her head down on the table at the thought of what that meant.

"Good, we have an agreement. Now would you mind fixing me and one of my men a snack? We'd be most appreciative. Cheese and crackers would be perfect. I'll watch to make sure you don't try anything funny." The smile on his mouth didn't quite reach his empty eyes. A chill ran down Paula's back as the impossibility of her situation settled over her.

Paula took a deep breath and began to reply when a knock rapped at the door.

"Are you expecting someone?" The man asked abruptly. He got up and looked toward the door, hiding from whoever waited outside.

"No." Paula replied. "Maybe my neighbor Lydia is checking up on me. She might have seen you around my house."

He growled nervously, "Get rid of her. Act like everything is fine. The fewer people who know we are here, the better."

Paula walked to the front door, looking at Christine on the couch who sat in a stupor. Two young men waited in the living room, one beside her and another sitting across from them in a side chair. She wondered where they had come from as she didn't see them when she and the heavy man had entered a few minutes earlier. Paula's heart broke as she wondered how long this nightmare would last.

When Paula opened the door, the familiar scent of jasmine and honeysuckle wafted inside before she saw who was standing in front of her. Holly waited before her with tears streaming down her face. With a knowing look but without a word, Holly and Paula hugged. "I'm so glad you're here," whispered Paula, hoping her voice wouldn't carry. "But what are you doing here? How did you know?"

"You asked the Father to send me, remember? I'm staying. I would have been here sooner, but I was detained by a prior engagement that became, well, a bit complicated." Holly leaned in and whispered in Paula's ear. "Merle and Gabe are standing guard in the driveway. You're safe." Holly brushed away the tears and transformed in an instant from the sympathetic friend to a fiery presence.

She barged in the house, motioning Paula out of the way and introduced herself. The two men with Christine rose to confront her. But they realized she wasn't intimidated and backed away. The heavy man glared at the pair of them from the kitchen, and they shrugged their shoulders.

"Lady Wisdom will be joining me during my stay. She's outside, walking around the neighborhood," Holly replied. She ignored the darts in the glances the two men threw at her as they attempted to stare her down but to no avail.

"Paula, you look like you could use some tea. Gentlemen, can I get you anything?"

"Holly?" The door opened and a short black-haired

lady walked in. She was older than Holly and wore her hair in a short bob. She was dressed casually in a lavender sweater, pink T-shirt, and jeans.

"Ladies, I think you are mistaken. Paula is dealing with family issues and asked us to stay with her for a while. Surely, you understand," one of the young men responded, glaring at Paula in a vain attempt to make them leave. His hair was long and straggly, and his beard was rather unkempt. The two women all but ignored his request.

"I'm sorry, I didn't catch your name, honey." Wisdom replied. "Holly and I are Paula's oldest and dearest friends, and we are planning to stay for as long as Paula needs us. We have first rights to be here. You, my son, are completely out of line, no matter the supposed family issues."

Turning to Paula, she said, "After Holly and I get settled, we would like to sit out in the garden with you and talk about your options. You had asked Father what to do a few minutes ago."

Wisdom looked over at Christine, who was beginning to come back to life on the couch. The other young man, Ricky, walked back over to her and helped her sit up. "How are you feeling, baby?" he asked as he put his arm possessively around her. He looked up at Wisdom. "What you do with Paula is of no concern to us. She does hold the cards in this situation, but other than that, you and your friend can talk with her as long as it doesn't affect us and our activities here." Christine began to weep and fell into Ricky's arms as he held her, comforting her.

"Bring my baby home, Ricky, please!"

"In the morning. Right now, you need another dose of my special tonic."

Paula watched in horror as Ricky began mixing up a concoction in a cup on the coffee table. He picked up a bottle of vodka off the floor and poured it in the glass. Paula moved toward the couch to knock everything over, but Wisdom blocked her path. "Let's go to the garden. My house is there now. You will stay with me."

"I don't have a garden. And your house is where?" Paula looked at her guest in bewilderment. She had never met this woman before even though she had just stated that they were old friends, but had no initial qualms about welcoming into her home as she was Holly's friend. But with these strange words, Paula was now having second thoughts.

"Follow me. What is happening here is very disrespectful to me and to what I stand for. Holly, however, loves this type of activity. She can move in the most complicated situation." Wisdom nodded toward Holly, who was now in the kitchen, putting a tea pot on the stove. "She will take care of the men and Christine."

Paula followed Wisdom through the kitchen as Wisdom opened the door to the back yard. Bile rose in Paula's mouth as the empty swing again reminded her of Sara. Paula glanced around, seeing the back yard through Wisdom's eyes, embarrassed at the mess. She didn't want this stranger to judge her on the lack of care of her property.

But when Wisdom opened the door and stepped outside, Paula gasped. Her dead lawn was gone and replaced with lavender now lining a path to a small house covered with flower boxes and roses dispersed among several herbs that grew around the cottage. The fragrant scent of the florals and herbs hung in the air, calming Paula's frazzled nerves. Patio furniture sat on the porch front of the cottage's living room window, looking as if it was paradise to a weary soul. Paula stepped back inside her home again look out the window next to the kitchen table. The scene was what she always saw: weeds and a small swing set among the uncared-for yard. She walked back to the door.

"How—"

"Wherever I go, my house comes with me," Wisdom replied as she took Paula's hand. "This is your safe place. The men inside cannot touch you here. In fact, when you come out here, they can't see my house through the window."

Wisdom guided her to the front porch the where they sat at the table. Paula looked over at her window into the house where the big man sat with Shaggy as Paula nicknamed the other young man. Holly came out of the kitchen door carrying a tray with a tea pot cups and cookies down the path to the cottage. She began serving the women tea. "Holly can see the cottage from the kitchen window, but no one else can."

"Wisdom helped me create a special herb blend this morning just for this occasion. I added some to the tea as you need these herbs at this time." Holly set the tray down on the table and sat down to the left of Paula as she still stared at the two men in the kitchen. They were paying no mind to the women outside.. Paula's cheeks flushed crimson as she struggled to breathe.

"Can they see us out here?"

"No." Wisdom said rather sharply.

"What do I do now?" Paula asked.

"You will listen to me and me alone, Paula," Wisdom replied. Paula looked to her left. "I will speak with the others who will be your companions."

"The others?" Paula asked.

"The angels who will protect you. You have to follow me as only I can bring you through."

"I want my granddaughter home right now. Can you make that happen?"

"That will be hard because of the evil of this situation. But let's discuss your options. You need to put a stop to this and take back ownership of your home. You need these men out of here now."

"But they will kill my daughter and granddaughter. I

can't allow that to happen."

"You are going to let them blame you for their actions?" Wisdom asked. "What they choose to do does not reflect on your decisions or the righteous actions you take. By letting them continue to stay here, you are protecting them from more evil that will befall them."

Paula sat back in her chair, her hands still shaking in fear. "So if I turn them in, what happens? Does Sara come home?"

"Only if we can find her. It all depends on the opposition that we face to get to her." Wisdom took a sip of her tea. "Thank you, Holly. This is wonderful."

Paula looked at Holly. They had been through many dark days together, and Holly had brought her through them, fixing the slightly bruised spot in her spirit. She trusted Holly. And if Holly trusted Wisdom and brought her here, she needed to trust Wisdom as well.

"Okay. Let's do it." Paula said. "How do I leave without them seeing me?"

"Close your eyes."

Paula obeyed, and when she opened them, she was sitting on a bench in front of the police station. She looked to her left and then right and laughed. Wisdom and Holly had joined her.

They walked into the lobby area and up to the counter. Paula explained what was happening in her home to the officer behind the counter. She felt Holly and Wisdom standing next to her even though the officer couldn't see them.

Although it seemed to take hours, the officer came back to the lobby where Paula waited after just a few minutes.

"We searched the entire house; it was empty, Paula. Your daughter and the men were gone. Nothing seemed to be disturbed. We found the drug items you mentioned lying on the floor by the couch as you described. But nothing—and no one—else was there. Christine and her buddies were gone. I'm sorry, Paula."

He took a deep breath and continued. "What you have told us is not uncommon."

——◆——

Marjorie sat on her front porch steps, drinking a soda and looking out across her yard. She enjoyed the warmth of the sun shining across the green yard and the slight breeze blowing from the north side of the house. The azaleas were done blooming, and she would miss seeing the bright red bush in the yard that had greeted her every morning for the last month as the blossoms faded. The Rhody in the front with its lush bright pink blooms replaced the azalea in late spring, and her roses on the south end would bloom soon.

Her mind raced, her thoughts many today. Her daughter was home now, working at a full-time job to support her family during her separation from her abusive husband. But her new boyfriend, Shaggy, made Marjorie uncomfortable in her own home whenever he came to visit. While he seemed friendly enough and offered to help out around the house, nonetheless Marjorie didn't like him. She couldn't put her finger on it, but he just gave her a bad vibe.

She wondered at her own reaction as these emotions were very unlike her typical response. She usually adored human contact. Just yesterday, she met a new neighbor, Judith, who was young and about her daughter's age. She worked out of her house as a home designer. Her flexible schedule allowed them to meet in the mornings for coffee to go over designs for Marjorie's bedroom.

Her husband had left her years ago. She had wanted to change the bedroom many times since then to help erase the difficult reminders of his presence. But raising her daughter on her own with no support from family brought many challenges. He didn't pay any spousal support or child support, so Marjorie took on a waitressing job at the local restaurant to make ends meet.

She had met her dearest friend Paula and Paula's husband Brad through her job. They came in for breakfast every Saturday morning. Paula invited Marjorie to church, and they regularly met to pray over their town and other burdens. Paula babysat Marjorie 's daughter while Marjorie attended nursing school and when Marjorie had the night shift..

Marjorie realized that they hadn't gotten together in a while and made a note to invite Paula to meet Judith to help welcome her to the neighborhood.

Marjorie rose from the porch to start dinner. The meat was already thawed out for tacos. Shaggy was coming over, and she planned to put him to work making margaritas and a salad. At least he wasn't pawing all over her daughter if she kept him busy in the kitchen.

Marjorie wasn't sure what he did for work. He never seemed to give her a straight answer. But whatever it was, he sure made a lot of money.

———— ♦ ————

Mike was sitting on the couch, eating the pizza he had ordered. He shared some with Sara. He made sure that she had fallen asleep quickly and moved her to the bedroom.

His good-natured attitude with kids hid the seedy side of the business and the cold calculating decisions that he made every day. His ability to convince any child to go with him—with or without the secret word—came in handy in this business. He thought, Ugh. Some of these guys who take these kids are such predators. At least I'm not like them. He wrinkled his nose in disgust at the thought of what they did. He had never been involved in any type of relationship with a child. But women were a different story. Before working for Boss Man, he'd been a pimp for almost ten years, selling women to men in the bigger cities. When Boss Man told him how much he could make selling children instead, he couldn't resist the temptation of all that cash. After working with some of the women he sold, he decided to offer drugs to doped-out people, especially mothers with small children. It was a win-win in his book.

His phone rang, breaking into his thoughts. "What's up?" he asked.

"Get the kid and move out. Now. Change of plans. I've got the mom, and we've left the house. Meet us at the compound, and we'll go from there."

Mike tossed his phone on the couch in disgust. When he was told that Christine lived with her mother, he knew this would happen. She was one of those praying grandmas, the worst in his line of business.

But he had promised to keep his word to Christine that no harm would come to her daughter. When he went to the bedroom and opened the door to check on Sara, the bed was empty. Mike's heart jumped into his throat. He checked under the bed and flung open the closet doors in a panic. Running outside, he lapped the entire house in record time, trying to catch a glimpse of Sara's blonde curls before finally leaning against the doorway gasping to take in air. He hung his head in defeat. He pondered what went wrong and how he would explain what had happened to Boss Man. Boss Man was very protective of his merchandise.

Then Mike's eyes narrowed at the thought of what he had lost. He would find Sara. There was no other option.

CHAPTER 2

Paula sat in silence on the way home. She walked in the front door as Wisdom followed and let out a loud wail. Holly entered the room as she cried and comforted Paula as the reality of the empty home hit her once again. Paula spotted Merle and Gabe outside at the entrance to the driveway. They had been with her when Brad died, providing comfort as she grieved his loss.

A few minutes later, Paula lit into Wisdom as she calmly sat at the kitchen table, drinking a cup of tea. "Why did I listen to you? Whatever possessed me to think this would work? They are both in danger now!" She pounded the table in frustration and then jumped up, unable to sit still any longer.

Wisdom patiently waited out the tirade, not saying a word. As Paula opened her mouth to break the unbearable silence, Wisdom stopped her.

"We did the wise thing, Paula. Never doubt that for a

minute."

"What do you mean? I will never see my granddaughter or my daughter again! How is that wise?"

"Was your daughter making wise decisions? What was she involved in? And the sale of your granddaughter to complete strangers—was that wise? You made a wise decision in going to the police as you took their illegal and even dangerous behavior to the proper authorities to correct. You are the only one here who is making wise decisions, Paula."

"But I put my family in danger," Paula sadly acknowledged.

"Their own unwise actions put them in danger. Your wise action did nothing but expose the lack of wisdom the enemy has. Trust me, it will work out to God's glory, to the peace you desire, and to the eventual good of all. Go to bed. We have a lot of work to do in the morning."

———◆———

Paula tossed and turned all night long as the walls closed in around her. No matter what she thought about doing, every direction seemed to be a dead-end. Holly had never failed her before, but she had only met Wisdom a few short hours ago. She wanted to ask Holly for a full explanation of Wisdom's plan, but Wisdom had said that Holly had other business to attend to that evening. That left Paula alone in her house with a woman that she felt more contempt for at the moment than any other woman she knew.

As the sky lightened in the west, bringing the promise of a new day, Paula finally gave up on sleep. She rose from bed and went in the kitchen to brew some tea. She was surprised to see that Wisdom was already up, sitting on the front porch of her house. Paula fixed her tea and went outside to join her despite her mixed feelings.

A few stars still twinkled in the pre-dawn sky. Paula followed the cobblestone path from her kitchen door to the porch and held back a laugh. I'm dreaming, she thought.

"You have concerns about me," Wisdom observed matter-of-factly. "It's okay. I would feel the same in your shoes. After all, I did just barge in and take over. And this is your daughter and granddaughter we're talking about."

"I guess that sums up my feelings," Paula replied as she sipped her tea from her favorite cup. Sara had drawn a picture of a cabin, and Paula had the picture put on the mug. Her eyes filled with tears at the memory. "Contacting the police has now put my family in greater danger than ever before."

"Paula, I have dealt with many scoundrels over the centuries. My house is located near the town square although I'm usually on assignment and not there often. My neighbors, Sanity, Knowledge, and Discretion, live just down the street. We work together to protect that which belongs to the Father."

Paula looked over at the swing that hung on the stately oak tree that Christine and her father planted when Christine was Sara's age. It had grown tall and strong and weathered many storms over the years. She nodded as Wisdom followed her gaze. "My granddaughter loved that swing. My husband put it up for her, and they spent hours playing out there as Brad pushed Sara. Their laughter echoed all the way to the street, making me smile as I went about my daily chores."

"He has such a great laugh," Wisdom replied.

"How do you know?" Paula looked at her strangely.

"You do remember where Holly and I live, don't you?"

Paula thought for a moment and smiled. "I know Holly has mentioned a cabin that belongs to the Father, but I never thought more about it. She took me there once, not inside the cabin but to the outskirts of the grounds. I know that it was built for Joshua's bride. I just caught a glimpse of the outside."

"And he will come for her one day. We are all anxious to meet her," Wisdom replied. "Several of the surrounding villages extend for miles. Your husband lives near my village and comes to visit every once in a while."

Paula wiped at her face as a tear trickled down her cheek. "I miss him," she said. "I never knew that when I visited Holly that I was that close to him. Why couldn't he see me?"

"He could. But sometimes the first few visits to heaven overwhelm newcomers a bit. Joshua asks family members to wait a while before approaching newbies.

"In a few days, we will take a trip there. I am working on a case right now for a courtroom in my village. The enemy can only enter the courtroom at specific times. We can face the principality that is holding your daughter and granddaughter hostage. I will walk you through the proper procedures of how to navigate the courtroom."

"A courtroom in heaven?"

"Yes. People lack understanding of the scriptures that the Father gave to His creation. It reminds me of the Tower of Babel the way it becomes translated.

"The Bible spells out the procedures to follow. They are very similar to those you use in courts here on earth. The difference here is that the judge doesn't know either of you when you go to court in this world. After he hears the case, he makes a decision based on witness statements.

"In heaven, the Father is our Judge, and he knows us inside and out—everything that we have done. His judgment is based on truth, which even the enemy knows. That is the difference, but as long as you agree with what the adversary says, it will go well with you."

"But the adversary lies!"

"He must be truthful in court, or he knows he will be held in contempt of court."

Paula pondered Wisdom's words for a moment. "Very interesting."

Wisdom smiled at her. "Heaven is beyond description."

Paula began singing a childhood song about heaven and roller skates and pearly gates. Wisdom and Paula laughed together for the first time in quite a while.

———◆———

Christine woke up to a dark room. The stale, musty smell told her that she was probably the first occupant in months. In the dim light, she couldn't even see if the room had any windows, let alone tell if it was day or night. She wondered where she was and how she had gotten here.

Her last memory was of the concoction Ricky had made for her at her mother's home. Home. Home felt so far away right now. She had blacked out after speaking harshly to her mother. A few fragmented memories of Boss Man talking with two of mom's friends tickled the edges of her memory. Boss Man's attitude changed once the pair of women had arrived. Although he argued with them, raising his voice, the women remained calm. Christine had secretly been impressed with the quiet authority they demonstrated.

Where was Sara? she asked herself. What had Mike done with her?

Now Christine couldn't even see her hand in front of her face, and her breathing grew shallower. She began to suck in deep breaths in an effort to increase her oxygen levels and stave off her growing panic. Somewhere in what she assumed was a house, a clock struck three times.

A draft tickled a stray strand of her hair against her face, and she rose from the bed to try and find it. She wanted to see if she could find a light anywhere.

Using the edge of the bed to guide her, she bumped into the wall. As she inched her way in the darkness, a familiar round object jammed into her hip. The doorknob, she thought. She moved her hand up the wall until she found the light switch. But she didn't want to signal her presence to anyone, so she left it off.

She tried the door. Although it was unlocked, it was heavy and seemed to be made of steel. No wonder the room was so dark. Pulling with all her might, she managed to open it a crack and peeked outside. The cool night breeze caressed her face, the air still damp after the evening rain. But then she jumped at the growl, and the telltale odor of wet fur assaulted her nose. She slammed the door shut and flipped on the light.

The dark gray room was furnished sparsely with just a bed and threadbare blankets that matched the color of the walls. The floor looked as if it had just been mopped. In other flop houses, drug items, such as syringes and needles, were usually strewn all over the floor. She was grateful this wasn't the case here as she glanced down at her bare feet.

While she knew she was held captive back at her mom's, Boss Man had taken it to a whole new level. She was used to being in control of her surroundings and could escape almost any situation. She knew where to get what she needed and, even more importantly, how to negotiate her way out of trouble.

Her memory was slowly returning as she lay on the bed, trying to think. Her past history included stealing from her mom—small items, such as jewelry, money, and knickknacks. But she didn't think her mother had even noticed. Later, her mother started hiding things from her. Her eyes misted over at the memory of the last item she sold.

Mike promised her that her daughter would be back by morning. But that was before her mother and her friends showed up. Boss Man had opened the door to the back yard and yelled at Ricky and Shaggy to grab Christine and move on out once the three women had left.

Her blood boiled at the thought of her mother reducing her to this. Everything had been going so well until her mother hid her treasures. Were those items really so much more important than Christine? She hoped maybe this one night might wake up her mother to what Christine needed. But she was the first to admit that she had no idea what would happen next.

———◆———

Marjorie knew she was taking a big risk. But her eight-year-old granddaughter needed her blue sweater before she left to go God knows where. She thought she could run home to grab it and be back at the police station in twenty minutes. That gave her plenty of time before they had to leave for the safe house.

She was so busy cursing her daughter's continued poor choice of boyfriends that led to all this that she forgot to pack the sweater. Imagine selling her granddaughter for sex so they could have drugs!
She dashed up the front steps of her house and looked in the living room window at the side chair right where the girl had left the sweater that morning.

Marjorie hurried, anxious to begin life in protective custody. The police warned that she would probably never return to the house where she had raised her children.

Marjorie carefully opened the door with her key. She walked over to the chair and grabbed the sweater, leaving the same way she entered. Her new neighbor, Judith, walked up the driveway as the door clicked shut behind her. She rushed by her friend, apologizing for her rudeness. "We'll catch up soon, I promise!" Marjorie called over her shoulder.

She barely registered the police car sitting across the street as officers regularly patrolled the area. But she instinctively knew what whizzed by her before she even heard the telltale bang—a gun shot. Too late, her jaw dropped as her friend fell at her feet. The officer swiftly pulled his car into the driveway, grabbed Marjorie, and shoved her in the back seat of the patrol car. He called for backup, announcing, "Officer down!" He barked at Marjorie, "Stay down."

From the floor, she peeked out the back seat windows as the officer waited for the ambulance and back up to arrive. She buckled in as he tumbled back into the vehicle. He sped toward the police station, lights flashing and sirens blaring.

"What do you think you are doing? Do you have any idea how much you have put at risk because of your foolishness?" The officer continued his tirade at Marjorie the entire trip to the police station, which took just a few minutes. By the time they arrived, her family was already gone.

Marjorie waited in the interrogation room, holding the small blue sweater in her hands. Paula arrived, groggy from a restless night's sleep.

"Seriously! You went back for a blue sweater? Do you realize what you've done?" Paula screamed at her. "We are not playing by the same rules anymore! You might never see your granddaughter again and all because of a blue sweater."

"Really, Paula? You have some nerve! My life has turned upside down. You have no idea of the trouble my daughter has caused me with her choice of boyfriends. She's brought those creeps through my front door and into my home. Until this morning, I thought my granddaughter was with her father. But no, the most horrible thing has happened."

"Wait. You too? My granddaughter has met the same fate. At least yours escaped." Paula looked over at her friend.

Marjorie's eyes softened a little as she saw tears forming in Paula's eyes. "Come stay with me and my friends. No sense in both of us living out these nightmares alone. Your family is safe but moving you there now will jeopardize all the work the officers have done."

"What about Judith, my neighbor?" Marjorie's eyes welled up with tears. "What's happened to her?"

"Oh, honey!" Paula replied as she took her friend's hands in her own. "She didn't make it. She died on the way to the hospital."

"No! She had just moved here a few weeks ago. We drank coffee together every morning."

"Judith was really an undercover cop. She moved in next to you as she was surveying your daughter's boyfriend. He's involved in trafficking up to his eyeballs. She tipped off the detectives working with her to keep you safe. If it weren't for her, who knows what would have happened?" Paula stopped for a moment and hugged her friend. "Come on, let's get you out of here. My friend Holly is a whiz in the kitchen, and I don't mind if she takes over in that department. She'll round up some food to help us forget our problems."

The page echoed in Doctor Jeffries ears. He knew who the supposed emergency phone call was from, but he wished he could ignore it. He leaned up against the wall, eyes closed, watching other doctors and medical professionals scurry past him to their duties. He nodded at a couple of them who stopped to question him about the persistent page.

He thought back to when he first started at the hospital. He had hopes and dreams and aspirations of a bright future ahead of him. While medical school was a challenge, his intelligence and determination saw him through the exhausting years of schooling. He took to his internship with the same intensity and focus. After he was hired, he gained tenure as one of the youngest doctors on staff. He enjoyed all the accompanying luxuries that his position afforded: a nice house with a three-car garage, several bedrooms, and a green and luxurious back yard. His trophy wife hosted expensive and catered parties every six months.

But once he succumbed to the advances of the young woman, he knew right away that it was a set up. He was trapped in a never-ending cycle of complying with Boss Man's demands.

He knew he had to take the call or risk losing everything.

He went to the nearest phone to answer the page.

The sharp voice on the other end got straight to the point. "We have a new location, and your equipment has been moved. You will receive an envelope within an hour with directions to the location. Come alone." Click. The caller hung up.

Dr. Jeffries groaned. One of the nurses asked him if he was alright. "I'm fine," he replied. "It's been a long day."

"Tell me about it. My doggies are feeling it big time today," the nurse observed as she walked off.

Two hours later, he was driving down a dark dirt road by a lake near his house. He knew about this place as he had helped his church build the camp for the kids to use during the summer. Now it was run down due to a lack of care, the facilities long since closed down. He hadn't been here in years.

When he arrived, other cars were in one of the parking lots by the main hall. He walked inside the lighted building and stood for a moment,looking around to get his bearings. Boss Man and Shaggy were sitting down at a table.

"Why did we have to move?"Doctor Jeffries asked as he looked for a chair.

"It was time. Someone donated this property to me." The smirk on Boss Man's face let the physician know that there was much more to the story. Boss Man had received many such contributions over the years, and the good doctor was just one of many trapped in his claws. To add to the irony when he was shown the make shift infirmary he would be working with a view of his lake house from the small window in the examination room.

CHAPTER 3

Sara sat at a small table, coloring. A stranger sat beside her and rubbed her back as she drew a picture.

"Is that a picture for me?" he asked. Her drawing of a cabin had twinkling lights all around it.

"No, sir. It's for me. It's my grandma's friend's cabin. I go there sometimes too." Sara moved away from the predator.

"Come and sit with me, and we'll draw a picture together. What should we draw?"

"We can draw my friend."

"What's your friend's name?"

"Joshua. He's very kind and nice."

"I'm very kind and nice too. Would you like to go get some ice cream later after we have some fun?" the man asked.

Sara turned and looked at him for the first time. He smelled funny and had dark black hair. He wore a Hawaiian shirt like her grandpa used to wear. But this man was nothing like her grandpa. Gamma would not like this man.

"No, thank you." Sara replied. She turned back to her drawing.

"Listen, kid. I'm trying to be nice to you here. You are leaving me no choice but to just take you with me."

"I'll call my friend, Joshua. He won't let you take me."

The man got up and picked Sara up by her arms. She began screaming in pain, and he let go of her and slapped her. Sara angrily looked up at him. "I'll tell Joshua!!" she screamed.

"Your friend Joshua has no idea where we are. And trust me you won't see any of your friends again to help you." He picked her up again, this time by the waist, to carry her upstairs. Sara began crying. Through her tears, over the predator's shoulder, Joshua followed them up the stairs. He whispered, "Come away from here with me, my child, and I will carry you for a while."

Sara saw herself floating out of the man's arms as Joshua wrapped his arms around her. As her body was being used, her spirit was unaware, safe in Joshua's embrace.

Once he finished with his depraved acts, the man left Sara in the room and locked the door. Sara sobbed into her pillow, the pain almost too much to bear. She thought she heard her name and turned her head to look up. Joshua knelt down beside the bed. He gently wiped the blood from her legs with the sleeve of his robe. With his other hand, he tenderly wiped the tears from her face. With his finger, he wiped away the bruise that was just starting to form on her cheek. Whispering in her ear, he called her his princess. And he promised to never leave her or forsake her. Sara carried that image through many tormenting events in the years to come.

———◆———

Nothing frustrated Wisdom more in this world than foolishness. She liked the word moron to describe how she felt about it.

She walked along Paula's property and out into the surrounding neighborhood. She passed homes with immaculate yards and shaped shrubs. Some driveways held the latest model cars with the fish symbol on the back bumper and even had boats stored on the side of the house.

Wisdom also noticed that many Christians refused to demonstrate responsibility when it came to the fish symbol. Everyone was in a hurry to relax, but when it came down to it, no one seemed to know how. "Sanity and Knowledge need to come for a visit," Wisdom remarked to herself as she continued walking. She arrived at Paula's house and entered to find Paula sitting on the couch.

"I heard about your friend," Wisdom said. "My friend, Sanity, is hovering over her now, and Holly is there as well. Marjorie will be fine although she will need some time to grieve the loss of Judith."

Wisdom went into the kitchen to fix lunch for her and Paula. Earlier that morning, she had gone to the cabin to see Joshua. She thought back to their conversation.

"I need some time in the court," Wisdom had told Joshua as soon as she arrived at the cabin.

"I will see my Father later today and set a date for you. Per the usual, I'll be there with you," Joshua said. They sat down on a bench on the front porch. "I was with Sara this morning. I so wanted to physically remove her from that hell hole," Joshua's voice cracked at the thought of what the little girl was suffering.

Wisdom reached over and grabbed his hand. "I understand. Unfortunately, we don't have permission to intervene so directly. The nature of the enemy and the choices of men prevent us from stepping in," Wisdom commented. "I feel the same way with Paula. Humans don't really understand what they see, which is hard on them. She knows she needs to trust me, but she still struggles. Their logic and ours differ vastly."

"They don't know how to truly apply my Word. They lack the knowledge to see what we do. When Sara saw me, her spirit ran into my arms. I could hear what the man was doing to her, which broke my heart, but Sara has no memory of it. Unfortunately, that will change in time as her trust bucket will empty, and she will forget me. She will believe the lie that I'm not helping her and that I don't even care. But I am limited by their free will, and until they turn from the evil they know, I cannot intervene the way they want me to. That's not how I operate."

"Someday they will understand," Wisdom replied. She brushed her hands across her denim skirt. "Meanwhile, we have to fight our adversaries in your Father's courts. "

Joshua got up and took Wisdom's hand. "Me thinks the world is rubbing off on you a little. You seem a bit out of sorts."

"More than that, the humans have no regard for what it means to be responsible. They are always out to get one another and drag them to court the first chance they have. And they then go before a judge who has no clue who they are without an advocate such as you. Yet they still expect a fair ruling. No wonder your Father stated they shouldn't take a brother to court. Neither would receive the justice your Father would give them when they come to him. He knows the depth of their hearts and will judge them accordingly."

"For over two thousand years, they have not truly sought after my Father's heartbeat. This is so sad as he will open every door to make sure they are free."

Wisdom now focused on Paula and poured two cups of tea for them both. She went to sit back down in the living room.

Paula thought that she was trustworthy and had opened her comfortable home to anyone in need of a place to stay. She saw a lot of herself in Wisdom. But it was as if her home wasn't hers anymore. She took a sip of the cup Wisdom offered her.

"This is your home, Paula. I'm not taking over. The issue is that it's not the world you once knew."

Paula blinked. She didn't realize she'd been staring at Wisdom and forgot that Wisdom and the others could hear her thoughts. Unnerved, she responded with a question.

"So what do I do with it now?"

"I think you know what you must do. You have an advocate with Marjorie. This home is a haven and completely protected from outside forces that would try to destroy you. You can do anything you want here to make it safe."

"There are more children involved?"

"Many, many more children. More than you could possibly imagine."

———◆———

For two weeks, no daylight entered Christine's room. The solitary light bulb had gone out three days earlier, trapping the odors inside with the darkness. She was more afraid of the dogs than the dark, so she left the door closed.

Ricky was her only connection to the outside world and brought her food and water along with the drugs she needed to keep from crashing. In small doses, the drugs helped clarify her thoughts, which made her situation better and worse at the same time. She sunk her head in her hands in despair. She was living in hell.

Thoughts raced through her mind. What have I done? Is Sara okay? Will she ever forgive me? And I put my mother and her friends in danger too. What are they doing now? Salty tears stained her pillow, which was wet from sobbing, until she was completely drained.

The door rattled and opened. The sunlight from outside blinded her, and the backlight kept her from seeing who entered the room. The dog growled outside but didn't come in the room with whoever entered. When the door closed, pitch blackness again enveloped them. The intruder swore and opened the door again to let in light.

"Boss Man sent me. You're coming with me. I've got a job for you."

"I don't trust Boss Man or you, for that matter." Christine replied as she scooted further back on the bed. She didn't see how close Shaggy was to her until he grabbed her and slapped her.

"I can easily sic the dog on you to chew you into a thousand pieces. But that wouldn't make me any money. Now get up!"

Christine rubbed her cheek while the man pulled her off the bed, half-dragging her out the door. She looked around at her surroundings, taking them in for the first time. Several cabins similar to where she had been kept were further across the complex. Every door was closed, and she wondered if her daughter was in one of them. "Saraaaaaaaa! Mommy is so sorry," she yelled, hoping her daughter might respond or at least hear her cries.

Her assailant slapped her again. "Shut up!" he snarled as he dragged her past the cabins to a large building.

Boss Man was sitting at a table when they entered. With only three chairs in the empty room, it echoed when they walked in. Her assailant plopped her down in a chair across from him. She looked at the man that had dragged her across the compound. He was tall and built solidly, dressed in jeans and a polo shirt. The coldest blue eyes she'd ever seen stared at her from somewhere behind the mass of long curly brown hair that matched his beard. She knew Shaggy's dark reputation from her earlier days on the streets and groaned. She turned to look at the man across from her. "What do you want with me?"

"Co-operation, for one." Boss Man said. "For starters, your daughter is not here, but she is being taken very good care of." His smirk told her more than any mother would ever want to know. A cry escaped from her throat, and she clawed her way across the table. Shaggy pulled her head back and slammed her in the chair. "You should know better than to cross me, you b*&#^!"

Boss Man stared at her, his face expressionless despite her outburst. "I've got a job for you. My assistant will be taking you to clean up. You'll be entertaining at a party tonight. If all goes well, we'll move you to a more comfortable room. If not, back to the cabin you go. It's your choice."

Christine looked back and forth between the two men. Neither option was what she wanted. She wanted to go home with her mother and daughter. But if she went to the party, at least she could escape that dreary room for a few hours. She made her decision immediately but waited for a few minutes to respond before slowly agreeing to go to the party. A plan formed in her head. "I guess I'll go to the party. I've got nothing better to do."

"Good choice. Now go get in the shower and clean up. Your clothes for the evening are waiting in there."

"I can shower by myself!" Christine said as she got up with Shaggy following behind.

"You might hurt yourself," he snickered as he continued to follow her.

"I don't need any help from the peanut gallery!" Christine entered the shower room and slammed the door. The door didn't have a latch, so she thought Shaggy might try to open it. Christine hurriedly changed out of her clothes and crawled in the shower. Her assailant had grabbed her wrists so tightly that they were starting to bruise. She knew her cheek was red from the two slaps she had received. She sighed as she knew she could look forward to more of the same treatment later that night.

She had only hooked up with a john once, but she hated it. If she knew where she was, she'd just leave. She had not only her location to worry about, but she also wondered what would happen to Sara if she left.

Her mother used to tell her that if she stayed in the shower long enough, she could solve all her problems. A random thought occurred to her now as she rinsed the shampoo from her hair. They had Sara. So it made sense that they had left her alone in a cabin. So why did they now need her as a prostitute? What happened to her daughter? She got out of the shower and wrapped a towel around her and went to the door.

Shaggy was standing there, smoking a cigarette. "You done already?" he asked.

"What has happened to my daughter? Where is she?" Christine asked. "Mike promised me she wouldn't get hurt." She looked at the big man sitting at the table as she spoke.

"You notice that I didn't make any promises of the kind. Just worry about the job at hand. Your daughter is being well taken care of." His repeated assurances did nothing to calm the knot that had settled in Christine's stomach since the day she had been taken.

———◆———

Doctor Jeffries walked into the makeshift medical unit, mumbling under his breath as he kicked at the tiled floor. His anger was directed more at himself than anyone else. He poured himself a cup of coffee to calm his nerves although he knew that the caffeine would make him edgy later. A few seconds later, Mike walked in from the waiting room.

"I got here as soon as I could. Is she all right?"

"See for yourself." The doctor opened the door, and Mike peaked in. A little girl was lying on her side in a fetal position on an examination table, whimpering in pain. Her blood-stained dress was torn in shreds, hanging loosely on her body. She can't be any older than ten, Mike thought, as he continued to survey the situation. Her long hair was matted in blood and another substance he couldn't quite make out. Her feet were bare and bloody and figured they were broken as well as other parts of her body. He shook his head in disgust.

The doctor closed the door. "When I agreed to providing the children with medical care, I didn't sign up for a john to beat the hell out of them. You told me that they would need vaccines and pills for STDs but not this."

"Do you know who did this?" Mike asked.

"No. She was at the front door of the clinic, lying in a pile of old blankets. As broken as she was, I thought I might hurt her worse if I carried her, but I knew that I had no choice. After all, I'm the only doctor on your payroll."

Mike ignored his comment. "Is she salvageable?" he asked.
"She'll walk again in time. I'm going to set her bones in a bit." He looked at Mike. "But don't try anything else with her. No one can use her like that anymore."

"What will happen if you do nothing? Will she die?"

"What are you saying, Mike?" the doctor asked in astonishment.

"You have rounds at the hospital. Go take of them. By the time you come back, she'll be gone."

"What on earth are you talking about? This is not what I signed up for. I took an oath, man. I'm required to save her."

"You are on our payroll, doc. If you know what's good for you, you'll walk away. But come back later this evening as we will have some girls who need a checkup. They have run into a little bit of trouble, and they need the problem taken care of. We can't take them to the next location in the condition they are in right now." Mike turned and walked out of the room without saying another word. Doctor Jeffries hung his head in defeat, ready to face the inevitable.

CHAPTER 4

Paula woke up with a start. Wisdom was standing at her bedroom door. "We have a court date." Wisdom said.

"When?" Paula asked.

"How soon can you be ready?"

"I guess I'm as ready as I'll ever be," Paula stated. "I'm very nervous."

"I've done this so many times that it's a walk in the park for me. But I can understand your apprehension. Your court system is nothing like ours."

"That's a relief! I am grateful that you're with me!" Paula replied. "Let's go."

As was the protocol, Paula closed her eyes. When she opened them she could see The Father's Cabin in a distance. She knew she was in one of the villages Wisdom had mentioned and immediately thought of Brad and wondered if she would see him once again.

"Not this time Paula. We have more important things

to attend to." Wisdom answered her thoughts.

As they walked, Wisdom explained the court systems to Paula.

"Heaven's courtrooms operate much differently than those on earth.

"For one thing, the Judge knows everything about the involved parties. This system was implemented before time, made so that the Father's creation could settle anything that was out of order. The first court recorded in heaven is in Zechariah 3:1–5 (MSG):

"'Next the Messenger-Angel showed me the high priest Joshua. He was standing before God's Angel where the Accuser showed up to accuse him. Then God said to the Accuser, 'I, God, rebuke you, Accuser! I rebuke you and choose Jerusalem. Surprise! Everything is going up in flames, but I reach in and pull out Jerusalem!'

"Joshua, standing before the angel, was dressed in dirty clothes. The angel spoke to his attendants, 'Get him out of those filthy clothes,' and then said to Joshua, 'Look, I've stripped you of your sin and dressed you up in clean clothes.'

"I spoke up and said, 'How about a clean new turban for his head also?' And they did it—put a clean new turban on his head. Then they finished dressing him, with God's Angel looking on.'"

When Paula entered the courtroom for the first time with Wisdom, her jaw dropped. The room was smaller than she expected with a table on the left with two chairs. On the right sat one chair. The judge's seat was missing, so the room looked different from other courtrooms Paula had seen on TV. Paula looked over at Wisdom. "The adversary sits there. Don't be afraid; he can't hurt you."

"I'm not afraid. Just overwhelmed." Paula explained as they sat down.

"All rise." Paula looked around the room but couldn't

tell where the voice came from. She and Wisdom stood. A door opened to their right, and a dark presence entered. Paula didn't know what to make of the presence. She couldn't see anything, but she coughed and sputtered at the stench, her eyes watering. There was no escaping the terrible odor. Within seconds, the fragrance of jasmine filled the room. Paula smiled at the familiar and comforting scent. Holly's here! she thought. . .

Wisdom interrupted her thoughts. "We won't see the Father. But we will hear his voice,"

Despite the lack of a judge's bench, Wisdom began her plea as if one were there anyhow.

"Your Honor, I have been on the earth and have seen a horrific event. You have said in Luke 17:2, 'It would be better for him if a millstone were hung around his neck and he were thrown into the sea than for him to cause one of these little ones to sin.' I would like a millstone put around this adversary for what he has been doing to children on the earth." She quoted from the ISV.

"Let me intercede for a moment, your Honor. I know a few things about Lady Wisdom's friend. She doesn't belong in your presence. She is a liar, a thief—"

Paula's mouth dropped open as the figure recounted her faults and crimes. Her face grew red, and she opened her mouth to speak when Wisdom put her hand over her mouth. "Agree to his words, or you will be in contempt of court," she whispered sharply.

"How do you plead?" the soft, loving voice surprised Paula.

She stammered, "I'mmm, uhhh, I'm guilty, your Honor."

The voice continued. "I hold you, Accuser, in contempt of court." The voice then addressed an angel that suddenly appeared in the room. "Go get Paula's book."

The angel left through a door that opened from nowhere to the left of the women, and he came back with a large book and gave it to Paula. "Open it," the voice commanded.

When Paula opened the front cover of the bulky book, the pages turned effortlessly. As she flipped through each page, they were all blank.

"What is this?" Paula asked.

"Your Book of Life. Each page is blank because every sin the adversary listed has already been forgiven."

"Wisdom, I have scrolls for you to take to the angels. Take them to the scribes to record first and then to the chancellor to seal." The voice addressed the adversary. "If you return to my courtroom, you will be held in contempt. Think about your choices if you go after Paula or her family. I know all about her daughter and her granddaughter. Your assignments against them have been canceled, and you are not welcome in my courtroom ever again in regard to this matter. Leave now!"

Paula watched as the adversary who had walked in so confidently just minutes before now shuffled out the door, head hung low.

Paula followed Wisdom out of the courtroom. The ground was soft and white, like powdered sugar.

They walked past a bench and up a walkway to another building. Paula pulled on the heavy door at Wisdom's request.

When they entered the building, they both walked up to a counter that separated them from several men, including John, the author of Revelation. The men sat at a long table, copying from scrolls they held in their hands into books before them. Paula looked around. They were the only ones in the waiting room.

"Wisdom! How nice to see you again!"

"Wonderful to see you again too, John. How are you doing?"

"We are busy. Several orders to record. Looks like you have quite a few with you."

"We do, and more will come in as I'm sure the adversary we met today will be back. It's a big challenge. Children are being sold on earth!"

"Nothing new since centuries before my time there, I'm afraid," John replied. "They were sacrificed to Molech in the Old Testament."

Paula gasped.

"I'm sorry. I should have realized that you had a guest." John replied. "I'll take your scrolls. Enjoy the coffee and scones. Holly brought them by earlier."

Wisdom looked at a photo on a wall and smiled. She had held several conversations with the man in the photo over the years. Although he was older, he wore the years well. His gray hair was slightly curled as it stuck out of his blue cap. His blue eyes were bright behind wire-rimmed glasses; his face wrinkled. But his smile made him look years younger. He still dressed in the trademark clothing of dark blue suspenders over a light blue shirt that he had worn on earth—still the same Charles that she had known from childhood.

"When did you get the photo of Charles?" Wisdom asked.

"His daughter brought him up to show him around. We loved having him here. He talked with us for hours about life in general. He made his daughter stay outside as he needed to take care of some personal matters."

"I know his daughter. She takes after him quite a bit. And I love his accent! What a great guy to have on our team on earth."

"Well, your scrolls are done," John observed as he put a cloth bag on the counter. "The chancellor is in, and you can take these to her to seal."

Wisdom and Paula finished their scones and rose

from their chairs. They thanked John and said goodbye, and Wisdom took the bag.

They left the building, and Paula discovered that the door felt lighter as they exited. They stepped again into the fluffy, white, powdery substance and walked to the chancellor's office down the road.

Her door was open, and Wisdom led the way inside. Paula didn't expect the room to be so much like the inside of Wisdom's cottage. It was small and quaint. The chancellor was sitting in a comfortable chair, wearing a plaid dress, drinking a cup of hot tea.

"Oh, Wisdom, how wonderful to see you again! And this must be Paula. I heard you were in the courtroom today."

Wisdom sat down on a couch across from the chancellor. Paula followed suit. Wisdom handed her the bag.

As the Chancellor opened the bag, tears began to flow down her face. She was a beautiful woman with striking young features. Her blond hair was pulled back into a bun, and glasses covered her brown eyes and sat on the lower part of her nose. She grabbed a tissue from the table next to her chair.

Paula looked around the room. She was out of tears, and pounded the table. The chancellor felt Paula's anger and looked at her. "It's okay not to cry," she said. Paula's face grew red at her outburst. The chancellor smiled at her.

The chancellor took off a ring and placed it in a bowl of warm wax sitting next to her as she sealed each of the scrolls. She tenderly took each scroll, read it, and then rolled it back up and sealed it. When she was done, she put them all back into Wisdom's bag.

"I know you will be back about this. It breaks my heart how many times I've seen this for thousands of years. Children are not slaves, garbage to be tossed, or possessions to be taken advantage of. I hope that they will be the last to come through here, but I know that they won't. I am working with some of our friends on earth who have been fervently praying along with those here in heaven who have prayed for centuries even before Joshua came to earth. Remember God's Word in Revelation 5:8: '. . . Each had a harp and each had a bowl, a gold bowl filled with incense, the prayers of God's holy people.'" The chancellor quoted from the Message bible.

She continued. "We will be holding a session in my courtroom soon, and Paula, you are invited to join us. This intense issue must be resolved."

"At least it's a start," Wisdom replied as she rose to pick up the bag. "We will hire angels to go to work for us," Wisdom continued as she motioned for Paula to follow her.

"Before you leave, Wisdom, let me set a seal on Paula's heart." The chancellor took her ring and placed it in the wax. She then rose from her chair and went to Paula. She placed her left hand on Paula's shoulder and took the ring with the wax, placing it on Paula's heart before Paula could say a word. Paula's heart played a tug-of-war within her as she struggled to put her emotions into words. She felt as if she were floating above her own body, watching as the chancellor placed the ring on her shirt and as the warmth of the wax entered her heart. The chancellor backed up to reveal a mirror behind the other woman. The seal on her heart was in the shape of a cross covered her heart and reflected in the mirror.

"Come back again just to visit, both of you. I would enjoy the company."

"Thank you, chancellor. When things settle down, we will return. I'll make cookies," Wisdom responded. She waited for Paula to come out the door, and they walked down the steps onto the soft, white ground.

As they walked through the short courtyard, Paula looked across a distant field. Suddenly, angels filled the courtyard. She tried to count but stopped almost immediately as they were innumerable. Wisdom stepped in front her and took the scrolls from the bag.

"This battle is fierce. I need angels with previous experience fighting the enemies in the human trafficking rings with the children. We need these children brought home. I need six angel teams dispatched as soon as possible. Who will set up teams for us?"

Six angels came forward. "We've battled them several times and have learned the techniques to win. We will be the team leaders," one announced as he took the scrolls and handed them to the other five. "The battle is so fierce because it involves children. Once the enemy has access to one, he does not want to let go. But they do eventually relinquish the child."

"Then you know what to do," Wisdom responded firmly.

"Yes, we do," The angel confirmed, and he gathered the group together and then flew off into the distance. Paula couldn't see them leave due to their swift departure. Wisdom bid them goodbye, and they turned around and walked back to a bench in front of the Scribes' Room.

"What do you think?" Wisdom asked.

"This is nothing like I've been through in the court system on earth."

"Angels can move in many areas and operate in ways that we can't on earth. Letters will find their way to places, and darkness will be exposed that has been hidden. Watch and see."

CHAPTER 5

Paula slept solidly for the first time in weeks. She had dozed and taken catnaps during since Sara and Christine went missing but refused to fall into a deep sleep due to the stress of the circumstances. The phone rang beside her bed, waking her now.

"Paula, this is Officer Grant. Can you come down to the station? We need to discuss a sensitive matter with you in person."

"Did you find my daughter or my granddaughter?"

"No, we did not, but we want to update you on the progress of the case. Bring Marjorie with you." The phone clicked as the officer hung up.

She rose and walked down the hall to Marjorie's room. Her friend's companionship helped her breathe more easily despite the challenging circumstances they faced. Marjorie might never see her daughter and granddaughter again although they were safe. Paula identified with missing her loved ones but had no idea where they were.

"Marjorie, Officer Grant just called. He needs us down at the station now."

Marjorie sat up on her bed and grabbed her bathrobe. "Have they—"

"Sadly, no. I'm not sure of the details. But we need to prepare ourselves. Let's pray."

The two arrived at the police station a half an hour later. They were taken into one of the interrogation rooms for security purposes.

Officer Grant was of medium build, cutting a handsome figure in his uniform. He often joked that his six kids and all their sports activities caused his graying hair. As he looked at the photographs he held in his hands, he only wished this child had been given the same chance his own children had. His wife had died from cancer ten years earlier, leaving him to raise the kids on his own. He struggled to grasp the enormity of the trafficking issue and how it affected each of the trapped children. Now grandmothers were grieving in another room. He gathered himself, sighing at the thought of facing the women.

"Ladies, I truly hate this. It burns at the core of who I am as a man and as a dad, let alone as a law enforcement officer and a lover of the Father. I can't fathom the person who would—" He fought to hold back the tears, but his voice caught as he took a seat.

"I can't show you any photos as you two are civilians. I can only give you a general description of what we found. A young child was brutalized and left for dead in a dumpster. I don't want to say more. I—" The husky officer's voice choked as he remembered the mangled images. The women gasped and started sobbing at his description despite his efforts to soften the blow of what he had seen.

Officer Grant took a drink of water to compose himself. "As officers of the law, we are supposed to show very little emotion, but these diabolical people are beyond the imagination. Do they even have a heart? I have dealt with pedophiles more than I'd like, but most of them are not capable of this much evil!"

"Where was this child found?" Paula asked through her tears.

"In a dumpster outside of town. I checked with the owners of the business, and they had nothing to do with it. But then again, how far does this go? Paula, you weren't the first to come in with your story. We've had several grandparents make similar reports, yet we've never been able to find these perpetrators. Marjorie, going home that day was the worst yet the best thing you could have done. Unfortunately, we lost an officer. Evidence shows that a high-powered rifle took Judith out, which tells us that these people mean business. I'm surprised that no one has tried to come after you yet, Paula. After all, you saw them."

"Let's just say that I'm well protected." Paula smiled. Officer Grant thanked her, thinking that she meant the police department, but Paula knew otherwise, referring to her heavenly protection.

"I still need to talk to the parents in the other room, but I don't feel ready. I know you two are prayer warriors. Will you pray for me now?" Officer Grant asked, hands stuffed in his pockets. "Telling survivors about the death of a child is bad enough but this . . . this—" His voice caught again at the horror of what the child had suffered.

"Of course." Paula reached across the table to pat his hand.

"Thank you" The lawman's gaze focused on Paula, and a look of acknowledgment registered in his eyes. He turned and left the room.

"Let's pray now," Paula said.

———— ♦ ————

Miles away, Sara shuffled along as she and several young girls were packed like sardines into a small cargo trailer. When one moved, everyone moved. Another young girl sat beside Sara and cried uncontrollably. Sara tried to comfort her as best she could. "It's okay. We will stop soon."

"Hey, princess! Where's your Joshua now? I've heard he's stuck like glue to you," a voice behind her taunted.

"He'll be here. He will protect us all."

"I've been on this route before," the voice mocked. "We won't be leaving for the next three days. Men come and go. Take the drugs that these guys give you. They will help you get through what's about to happen."

Sara began weeping quietly.

CHAPTER 6

Christine knew that Sara was in deep trouble. But trying to attack the junkie that waited outside the shower would not be the wisest move. He roughed her up, stabbing her in the thigh and leaving a cut. Boss Man wanted Christine safe and in one piece. As punishment, he locked up the junkie in one of the cabins and sent Christine to the makeshift infirmary where another of Boss Man's thugs attended to her injury with surprising kindness. She was then sent back to the same cabin where she had been held hostage for weeks.

Once back in the dreary cold cabin, she cried, more alone than ever. If she tried to sleep, she had nightmares. Boss Man had now cut off her drug supply, and she was fading fast. Weeks had passed since that refreshing shower, and her once clean hair was again scraggly and oily. She wondered if anyone thought about her or if they would ever find her.

As she lay in the half-state between sleeping and wakefulness, a demon appeared over her. But once she screamed, it left.

In the cold dark room, she thought again about trying to sneak out the door. Boss Man had cut her food supplies as well, which was now taking a toll on her. She was beginning to suffer from malnutrition and was almost ready to eat the rats that scurried around at night if she could just catch one to kill it. Where had everyone gone? It had been too quiet in the last few days.

She rose from the bed and walked to the door. She thought she saw a light flicker behind her and turned around. A table now sat in the middle of the room with one candle and real food. She thought for a moment that she might be hallucinating, but she could make out a transparent face in the dim candlelight. Is this another demon already? she wondered. But she sensed a peace she had never known before at the vision of this face—like she could really trust this being.

"Who are you?" she asked, her voice scratchy from thirst and disuse. She hadn't spoken in days, and the sound of her own voice surprised her.

"My name is Holly. And I brought you some food and something to drink. Come sit."

"Did Boss Man send you? How did you get past the creeps outside? How did you get in without me noticing?" Christine realized the question was pointless as she'd been given drugs before she was thrown back in here. She still wasn't really able to focus on her surroundings.

"I love to visit dark places to bring light. It doesn't get much darker than this. Come and eat. Help is on its way. But you need some strength first. "

Christine didn't need much encouragement to do what Holly said. She sat down at the table, filled with her favorites: bowls of soup, various fruits, and tea. "Do you work for Boss Man?" Christine asked as she sipped some broth from one of the cups. The warmth of the tasty soup nourished her as she drank.

"No. I go where I'm needed. You've been mostly weaned from the drugs they had you on," Holly informed her as she moved to the makeshift bed. Christine looked over at her bed where Holly sat. It was covered with the torn blanket as well as possible. Spots of dried blood from the stab wound that Shaggy had inflicted months ago still covered the mattress. "You seemed to be in a place of no return."

"What do you mean?"

"You were spiraling downhill pretty fast. You made some decisions along the way that hurt quite a few people."

"But what now? I don't know what to do. I can't leave. I have no one else. There's no way out."

"You're right," Holly replied as she poured a cup of tea for Christine.

"Where can I go?" Christine asked.

No sooner had the words came out of her mouth when the door burst open. A bright light flooded the room and blinded Christine. The officer put his gun back in the holster and bent down in the chair to Christine's level. "Officer Grant! I found someone here! I think it's her!" He picked up Christine's frail body from the chair.

Christine turned her head to see Holly mouth, "I'll see you soon." She disappeared as quickly as she had appeared just moments before.

The officer looked around the room as he backed out of the door carrying Christine. He followed her gaze to the empty chair and rickety table. She focused intently on the chair as if someone was sitting there. But he saw no one else in the dilapidated room. Who knows how much longer she would have survived if they hadn't arrived when they did? Damn the person who had left this young girl to die alone in this hell hole.

Officer Grant sighed and prayed for another breakthrough. One was coming that he would not anticipate in his wildest dreams.

Six months later

Mike was on his way out of town. He was checking out a few new recruits. The rain was heavy due to the storm, but he was used to driving in it. The road he was traveling on was not well used as he usually found side roads when he needed to hide. He flicked up the classical music station louder. He thought it fit with his surroundings.

Suddenly a flash of light hit the hood of his car. He jumped from the shock and took a few seconds to regain his composure. He blinked but couldn't see a thing. He frantically rubbed his eyes and instinctively slammed on the brakes.

A voice boomed over the radio. "Why are you hurting my children, Mike? Don't you know I could put a millstone on you and toss you into the sea?"

"Who are you?" Mike panicked. "Can you help me?"

"I will help you. But you need to honor me. I am above all things."

"Who are you?" Mike asked again, his heart in his throat. "I can't see, and I need help."

"Mike, help is on the way. My friends will take care of you."

"Is this who I think it is? I suppose I am at your mercy," Mike responded weakly.

"You are."

Weeding was not her favorite job but Paula was diligently working in her front yard, her eyes burning from endless tears mixed with pollen.. She thought back to her visit with Officer Grant weeks ago and what he had said and that mysterious look that he gave her as he left the room. She thought it had to do with the frustration of the issue that drug raids almost seemed to be a thing of the past as human trafficking took over. But realized it was more.

Wisdom came out of the house with a tray of tea and cookies, joining Paula on the steps of the front porch.

"We have another court date," Wisdom informed her as they sat together.

"What needs to be done? Whatever it is, I'll do it."

"Mike is in my cottage. I want you to go talk to him."

"Let me at him!" Paula responded, her eyes blazing. She jumped up from the step, rushing toward the front door. Wisdom's stern voice stopped her. Paula glared at her.

"Wait a minute. Mike is blind. But he has heard from Joshua and realizes what he must do. When you go to him, you are to help care for him until his eyesight returns," Wisdom replied.

"And we lose the court date if I don't?" Paula asked angrily.

"Talking to Mike and guiding him and teaching him about the Father will help the situation. We can take him with us."

"Why would we want to do that? Mike sold my granddaughter, and who knows where she is! And my daughter is in the same situation, for that matter. The last year of not knowing where they are has been hell, and he is at fault."

"Mike has repented of everything he's done. Once his eyesight returns, he will apologize and help you. You need him on your side, Paula. And we need to take him to court so that the adversary will leave him alone."

Paula leaned back on the step. She wanted this night-mare to end. Three weeks ago, Sara turned six years old. Did whoever had her know that and make her feel special or even acknowledge her birthday? What about Christine? She thought back to all that had transpired over the last few months.

"All right, I'll do it." Paula replied begrudgingly. "Can Officer Grant come? He's been so helpful in recent months. I'm sure he will want to join us."

"No. Joshua needs him here for other duties."

————◆————

When Paula walked into the kitchen, she stood at the back door, looking out to the back yard. She again watched the tree with the swing floating in the breeze. Officer Grant now regularly mowed the lawn, but Paula now called him Ray. That mysterious look he had given her that day had turned into coffee, a meal at her home, regular visits, and even actual dates. She often went over to spend time with the kids as well and to cook for them. She enjoyed the calm stability that their relationship brought her. Paula fell in love with his kids as well. Ray admitted he had his hands full with his youngest, the thirteen-year-old girl.

She wondered now how Ray would act if he knew that Mike was now in Wisdom's cottage. This was the break in the case they had been waiting for. Mike's recovery had opened a new door, and despite the circumstances, he could prove to be an ally.

Paula entered the her house and walked into the kitchen. She opened the kitchen door to the backyard.. Wisdom's cottage was just a few feet away. Paula laughed as she stepped on the cobblestone walkway. She would miss it when Wisdom returned home.

Standing on the front porch, she took a deep breath. She wanted answers but knew they would not come today.

The plan was to show Mike what his new life would look like with Joshua as his friend. She questioned why Joshua wanted to be a friend to Mike of all people after everything that Mike had done.

A slight breeze caressed Paula's face through the open cottage door as she entered. The blindness had heightened Mike's other senses, and he sensed her presence even in his dark state. She walked into the living room where Mike sat and went and laid hands on him and prayed without hesitation.

Mike blinked for a few seconds. The blurry room started to come into focus. The presence of the older lady standing over him praying relaxed him. Or maybe her prayers calmed him; in any case, he knew that she made a difference. When Paula was done, she sat down on a couch across from him, scrutinizing the man whom she wanted to despise with everything she had.

"You're Christine's mother," he observed after a few minutes of companionable silence. He began weeping uncontrollably with his head in his hands for almost a half hour. Paula waited, praying quietly in the Spirit under her breath.

As he slowly regained his composure, he sat up. Tears still streaked down his unshaven face. Paula rose to get a cool cloth to help dry his tears. "Let's go get your babies back," he announced as he accepted the cloth from her.

<hr>

Wisdom and Holly sat at the bistro table on the front porch of Wisdom's house while Ray rested on the front step.

"Okay, are you telling me that I cannot go into your house and arrest the one man that could break this case wide open? And in addition to that, my girlfriend is in there right now, praying for him!" His eyes blazed as he fumed,his body glued to the porch step, he couldn't move, but even that didn't irritate him as much as know he had no control of the situation. He could scarcely grasp the fact that just twenty feet away was Paula's back door. He had mowed the lawn yesterday and hadn't seen "Wisdom's Cottage" then. "You are harboring a fugitive. You know that, right?" Even as he spoke, he wondered if the statement was true at this point. He shook his head at his own thought.

"By your laws, Ray. Here, have a cup of tea. Put these drops in it. They will help you calm you down so that you can take the next step." Holly handed him the blue vial with the label, "Anger Management," on it.

"And that would be?" Ray stared at the cup of tea. He shrugged his shoulders and used the dropped from the bottle and put drops in his coffee.

"He has a court date with the Father today, and we are going to join him and Paula."

"What court are you talking about? This isn't the Middle Ages. He needs representation and a jury of his peers."

"So you believe he is innocent?"

"Not by a long shot."

"The Father knows the truth. That is the court we are going to." Wisdom replied.

Ray looked at Wisdom. "Then can I have him?"

"Certainly. He is still under the authority of the courts on earth for what he has done."

The man looked around. The reality he knew had shifted in only a few minutes. He trusted these women as he knew they were Paula's friends, and he thought they were responsible adults for the most part. Even so, this was a new arena, and he wasn't sure he could handle it.

Wisdom sensed Ray's doubts. She rose to sit next to him. "Close your eyes." Her voice was soft but firm.

He listened. When he opened them again, he was sitting in a courtroom with Wisdom seated next to him. "What is—"

"We're in heaven's courtroom. We are just observing," Wisdom whispered.

In front of the officer was the defendant's table with Mike, Paula, and Holly seated there. He started to say something but couldn't get the words out. He stammered, "What . . . I . . ." before he simply closed his mouth and watched. The door to the right opened, and a slimy figure entered with his underlings behind him. The creepy being, which reminded him of something from a horror movie, took his position at the prosecution table. His minions sat behind him.

When Ray looked ahead to the front of the courtroom, there was no judge's bench. It was as if he were looking into a cloud.
An authoritative voice bellowed from the cloud. Despite its strength, the officer felt peace. He had trouble comprehending so many aspects rolled up into the one sound.

"What are your accusations toward the defendant?" The voice boomed and echoed throughout the courtroom yet only seemed to be a thought in the lawman's head.

"Your Honor, the defendant is a criminal in every respect of the word and should be prosecuted to the fullest extent of the law. You have stated that a millstone should be tied around the neck of one who harms a child, and I hope you have one ready," the alien announced. He looked at Mike as if he were already condemned and ready to be thrown into a watery pit.

The miscreant continued, "The defendant has been buying and selling the children, those so precious in your sight, to the most depraved humans who also have further abused them and taken away their innocence. His underlings have even murdered babies when these children became pregnant by these vial acts of monsters. I expect the whole extent of the law to be imputed against this man."

As the monster sat down, the voice addressed Mike. "And how do you plead to these charges against you?"

Everyone in the room held their breath, waiting for his response. Then the underlings smirked at each other, giving each other high fives. They knew what Mike's fate would be: to become their tenant after Officer Grant saw to it that justice was executed in his case on earth. They looked over at the law enforcement officer, nodding and smiling as if they were on the same team. They would wait their turn to get their grubby paws on him. They knew earth's laws, and Mike didn't stand a chance of survival once the word got out about what he had done. The creepy beings would be sure to tell their comrades in the earth's prison system about his crimes.

Officer Grant was smiling as well. He knew that he was right. With these accusations, the Father could never even consider Mike to be one of his own.

Mike took a deep breath as he stood still. Paula stood next to him. "Guilty as charged, Your Honor."

The underlings roared and cheered as the Alien walked across the front of the courtroom, high-fiving each one in turn. They huddled together, their chatter excited until the door opened. Joshua entered, wearing a white robe with a red sash across his right shoulder. His feet were bare with deep scars through them. He raised his hand so that everyone, especially the underlings, could watch what he was about to do. The room suddenly grew quiet.

"Father, I stand before you as a propitiation for Mike's sins that I took on the cross for him over two thousand years ago. He is completely forgiven!"

"Yes, my Son. He is forgiven." The booming voice echoed through the room, addressing the crowd, but especially seemed directed at the underlings and the slimy being. They fell back in their chairs in defeat and despair. "Should I ever see any of you here speak another word against this man regarding today's events, I will hold you all in contempt of court."

Several scrolls appeared on the floor at Joshua's feet. The underlings shrieked in anguish, anticipating what that meant. The bailiff went to their row to eject them from the court along with the adversary.

When the door slammed shut behind them, Joshua bent down to pick up the scrolls and laid them on the table where Mike, Paula, and Holly were sitting. "Take these to the scribes and then to the chancellor. The angels will be waiting for you for their assignments."

Wisdom rose from her seat as Officer Grant followed. His stomach flip-flopped at what he had seen. He had no idea what the scrolls meant, but the voice in the cloud intrigued him. He had heard the Father before but never like this. Despite the depth and intensity of the voice, compassion rang through every word. Ray could tell how much the Father loved Mike and that it pained the Father to pass judgment on him. Ray now questioned what he need to do as an officer of the law on earth. Yes, Mike was guilty, but yet the law man needed him to help save the children that had been taken.

Officer Grant listened as Joshua picked up the scrolls and handed them to Mike. "You have to go on a journey yourself now. The world will not be kind to you because of the previous choices you have made. They will judge you and even torture you because of it, even more so because of the grace you experienced today. My friends, Merle and Gabe, will be with you from now on. When the underlings return to harass you, they will see them with you and then leave you alone. These guardians will protect you."

Mike broke down in tears, overwhelmed at all the Father had offered him. He looked up at Joshua. "What are the scrolls for? What do they contain?"

"These are continuing orders from Paula's request when she came here several months ago. What has transpired with you has opened closed doors. The angels that were assigned to Paula had scrolls as well. One was finally able to break through to you. That changed everything. You can now move freely wherever you need to."

"But I have not been in contact with anyone for three days, Joshua. Before this, the longest I've been out of contact was only a few hours. Even if I went on vacation, I always touched bases with the Boss Man. They know something is up as my phone was blowing up with texts and phone calls."

"Awww. That's simple. When we finish with everything today, you will be back where we found you. I can work around time. It is of no consequence to me." Mike looked in front of him through the cloud. The scene of him driving on the road with the car stopped replayed in his mind. "My car was hit by lighting. It won't run."

Joshua laughed. "Is there anything I cannot do? You will still continue as before. But you have to make a choice. What will you do with the child you planned to pick up?"

Mike looked at the scene in front of him, surveying the damage to his SUV. He thought about the cost to his vehicle, his baby. Yet he had transferred other people's babies—living and breathing children—to a life that made them lose their innocence. His eyes teared up yet again. "If I do this, someone needs to take that child and protect her. I can't give her to that monster."

Grant spoke up. "Give me the name and address of that animal, otherwise known as your contact. We will take care of him quietly. But you will still be paid. Depending on where the child is coming from, we can help the parents too." Officer Grant looked over at Joshua. "I want to know how to do this so that I can bring those that are entangled here also and help free them. I know it will be hard."

"Ladies, let's take Mike and the officer on a field trip, starting with the court of scribes. I'll join you," Joshua said as he threw his arm around Mike's shoulders. Together, they walked out of the courtroom.

Officer Grant looked at Joshua when they left the courtroom. "I have some things I need to set in order back in my office. If Wisdom will come with me and help I think we can return in a while."

"Certainly." Wisdom responded. "It won't take long."

CHAPTER 7

Christine startled at the unfamiliar noise. She sat up in her bed and looked around her room, smiling and reflecting at how far she'd come in the past year since the incident in the dark cabin with the creepy shower.

Christine climbed out of the luxurious bed and grabbed her robe. She went downstairs for a cup of coffee.

The safe house where Sergeant Grant had hid her was beyond her wildest dreams. While she longed to go home, the officers told her it would be the first place Boss Man and his thugs looked. She knew that she would be safer hidden away until those who had taken her and her daughter were caught. She was still a target for the trafficking ring and knew too much about what the Boss Man was doing and about his operation. Christine finally realized that the ring was much bigger than she had previously known.

Now that she thought about it, she realized that the

increasing isolation in the room and the lack of food told her one thing: Boss Man and the junkie had taken the other girls and left her there to die. The doctor that Sargent Grant had brought with them when she was rescued gave her anti-anxiety medications to calm her down. The lawman couldn't—or wouldn't—tell her where Sara was, either.

She told the officers everything she knew in exchange for a lighter sentence. The prosecuting attorney and judge took the fact that she was actually a trafficking victim into consideration when sentencing her. The separation from her family and the punishment she endured when captured was enough of a sentence, according to the authorities. Even so, the luxury that surrounded her didn't help address the constant emotional pain she lived with, knowing what she had done. She was now completely free from drugs, and the others living with her were health nuts, in her opinion. Yes, her mother gardened, canned, and stocked up on homegrown produce, making soups from her garden treasures, including the mushroom hunting her father and Christine had done before he died. She cherished those times even more as the memories came to the surface after years of drug use.

Her housemates, professors at the local community college, had left a note on the kitchen table. They had an early class that morning but would be back soon.

The officers assigned Christine a new name, Natalie. Part of her cover story was that she was a distant cousin of the professors. Natalie was quiet and reserved with only these cousins left as her family. Many women had walked through their doors over the years, and no one ever questioned any of their supposed relatives. Her hair was now a dark auburn, no longer the blonde she had loved. Even her contacts were tinted blue and hid the brown eyes she was born with. After coming off the drugs, she had gained a healthy weight over the last several months. She often ate alone due to the schedule of the two teachers.

Natalie insisted that she now be allowed to attend classes and earn a degree. She was aware of the risks involved. She wanted to major in psychology and felt it would come in handy someday. Still Sergeant Grant repeatedly denied her request.

Sergeant Grant was adjusting to his new position. At least, that is what Christine thought as he kept refusing to grant her request. He saw no reason to give into her demands and place her at further risk of exposure.

Until this morning. The phone rang, but Christine ignored it per her instructions to never answer it. She listened as the voice mail picked up.

"Natalie! If you are there, pick up!" Sergeant Grant's voice boomed with excitement.

"Good morning. What has you all chipper? Is it Sara? Have you found her?" He inhaled sharply. Her questions tired him out, but he knew that she deserved answers.

"I found a four-year scholarship for you to go to school! I'll fax over your paperwork this afternoon. You got your wish!"

"Sergeant! Thank you. But what changed your mind?"

"Christine, have you ever visited a friend named Holly before?"

Christine was taken aback by the use of her given name. "My name is Natalie. And yes. I have met Holly but in my imagination or maybe in hallucinations." She took a sip of coffee. "Why?"

"It's a long story. I'll share more later." Officer Grant wasn't sure he wanted to share his experience with her just yet. He felt overwhelmed by what had happened with Mike, in the last few hours. He had worked everything out so Mike was now working with the department to help organize a task force to save the children in trafficking situations. The plea agreement with the district attorney was approved and granted. He chose to not tell her about Mike or to tell Mike about Natalie. "Anyway, I have pulled some strings and got you a scholarship. Use it wisely." He hung up the phone.

Natalie sat back in her chair. She reflected on her experience at the dark cabin. Holly had really been there! If Sergeant Grant knew her too, then she had to be real, and what happened was real as well.

Natalie thought back further still to the conversations she had had with her mom over the years about someone named Holly. But she had thought her mom meant that Holly was all in her mind, similar to the adult version of an imaginary friend. Still, she remembered a sweet woman who lingered around, almost as a shadow, after her mom lost her brother to cancer. Three years later, the same shadowy figure returned after her father died. She didn't understand the grief her mother was going through even though she was experiencing the same emotions. But mother and daughter processed their grief much differently; her mom withdrew and became quiet while Natalie just rebelled further.

Natalie was pregnant at the time and blamed her mother for keeping her father from her when she needed him most. To this day, the boy who got her pregnant had no idea that he was a father although she saw him often around town. She needed money for a bus ticket to anywhere but home. She knew that he would help her as he had many times in the past. What she didn't realize was that in nine months, a child would change her life as a result of that one action, adding a huge responsibility to her young shoulders. Her connection with the baby's father would now be set forever. Her father had died while she was still running from herself.

The kitchen door opened, breaking Natalie's train of thought. One of her roommates walked in. Tonya was a mathematic whiz and one of the top professors in the state in her field, but she opted for the community college atmosphere and the warm feeling of their small town. In this way, she could do what she really felt called to do—take in those like Christine whose lives were affected by pedophiles.

"How is your morning going?" she asked as she poured hot water into a cup and added a tea bag. She took out a carton of almond milk and poured some in her cup.

"Surprisingly well. Sergeant Grant just called. He found a full four-year scholarship for school for me. I can finally study psychology."

"Awesome!" Tonya replied. "Will he let you go to the university near here?"

"I didn't ask. I was too excited. Still no word on Sara." Natalie's enthusiasm dropped, and she tried to hold back her tears as she thought of her missing daughter.

"I understand, and I am sorry." Tonya answered. She looked at her friend and made a suggestion to help get her mind off her problems. "Let's head into the city, do lunch, and grab a course catalog. We'll even do some window shopping and find what we like at the thrift stores."

Natalie smiled. "That sounds fun," she agreed as she rose from her chair. "Give me fifteen minutes to dress and get ready for the day."

———◆———

Mike and Sergeant Grant followed Joshua as he walked on what looked like a glass sea. Below them was the earth, flat as a pancake, not round. Mike and Sergeant Grant looked at each other in wonder. Joshua anticipated their questions. "Yes, the earth is round, but I have made it flat so that you can see what I want to show you." He bent down and pointed to a small spot on the globe. Mike watched it suddenly expand and zoom in on the house where he was supposed to take Paula's granddaughter. With tears in his eyes, he glanced back at the three women on the bench behind him. "Don't let her see this, Joshua."

"This is for you and for Sergeant Grant," Joshua reassured him. The lawman looked at Mike and put his hand on his shoulder. He looked over at Joshua and nodded. "Go ahead." Joshua bent down as if to pull the earth closer to them, reminding Sergeant Grant of the crime shows on TV where the computer screen became larger just by swiping it. Suddenly, they were standing in the corner of a room in the house. Joshua was not there.

Sara was lying on the bed, tied to the bed post. The sergeant ran over to her, but his hand went through the scarves that bound her, and he couldn't untie them. At the same time, Mike tried to undo the other scarf on the other side with no success. "What do we do?" He looked at Sara, who was drugged.

The door opened and a large man entered with a length of rope, a Billy club, and some other unusual paraphernalia. Mike moved closer to him in order to protect the girl. But Mike walked right through him as if he wasn't there. He stared at Sergeant Grant in horror. "We have to stop him!" The man didn't turn around or acknowledge the pair. He beat Sara and did unspeakable acts to her while she lay there in a comatose state. Mike and the sergeant tried to grab at him, but he slipped through their fingers. When the man finished, he left the room, closing the door behind him. He didn't bother to look back at the devastated figure on the bed.

The door opened again, and Joshua walked in. A shadow snuck in and entered Sara as she slept. Mike and the sergeant looked over at Joshua, the questions on their faces. "It's her spirit. It leaves her when someone commits these vile acts against her." Joshua bent down to untie her from the bed post. He patted her bruises with the hem of his robe, softening their appearance before they formed. Within seconds, they were back at the Glass Sea.

"Joshua! Take us back!" the lawman exclaimed. "We need to save her!"

"Oh, that I wish you could!" Joshua cried, tears running down his face. "But there is so much work to be done before you can reach her."

"What do you mean, Joshua? She's right there!" Mike asked.

"Yes, she is, Mike. As are many, many other children you have sold to men and to women. But the enemy used a process to get her to where she is now. And it will take a process to save her and the others."

Mike and Sergeant Grant looked at each other in confusion at Joshua's words. They looked down at the Glass Sea. An ocean of turquoise water spread across the earth. The image of Sara and all they had seen was now gone.

They turned and looked at Joshua as he walked from the sea back to the bench where the women sat. Mike stood with his hands on his hips. "Joshua, I don't understand. I thought that your Father was in control of everything. If that's the case, why did you leave her there?"

"What did you want me to do?"

"Save her. You could touch her and untie her. You stopped the blood. But then you just left her there in that monster's house! You could have gotten her out! What happened? Why did you leave her there?"

"Mike, how did you come to know me?"

Mike thought back to a few days before. "Through my radio when my car died."

"Did I control your decision to come to me?"

"I was blind and desperate. And I could have been there for hours. Even my cell phone died."

"You didn't panic. Why?"

Mike though a moment. "You were kind. I felt safe."

"But did I control you?"

"No. I followed you, just like you asked. I didn't know where I was going, but I just knew that wherever it was, it would be better than where we had been."

"How did you know that you could trust me? You only had my voice to guide you."

"I just knew."

"And what did you learn? Did I control anything?"

"No. It was all my choice."

"And when you go back, it won't change. You will be back in your car. You will have a choice to make—continue with how you have lived your life or work with law enforcement. The decision is yours."

"We have worked out a plea agreement.," Sergeant Grant explained. "It's totally up to you if you want to work with us to save these kids."

"I deserve everything coming to me on earth. How will it help anyone if you arrest me?" Mike paused for a moment, growing serious.

"The plea agreement was granted as the information that you have is very valuable to this case." Sargent Grant answered.

"Whew, that's a relief. Okay." Mike's attitude changed again. He shuffled his feet, angrily kicking at the ground. "I can't get those images out of my mind. I can't let what I saw ever happen again to another child. That's why I will agree to be a confidential informant."

"Let's schedule our upcoming meetings to finalizing our plans. But after what I saw today, I couldn't ask for a better partner. Let's get our kids back."

CHAPTER 8

The next moment, Mike was back in his car, driving down the road as if the last week had not occurred. The music was playing on the radio. Usually, nothing fazed him, including his job. But after meeting with Joshua and Sergeant Grant, his nerves were a bit rattled. As he drove down the road, his cell phone rang. He pushed a button on the visor above him, keeping his eyes on the road.

"Mike here."

"Mike, are you on your way?"

"About twenty minutes out. What's up?"

"Our girl isn't going to make it. She's too far gone. Boss Man wants the baby, so we are going to bail. The girl is passed out in her room. I don't know what state she'll be in when you arrive. The baby is in a dresser drawer, sitting on the floor. Boss Man said for you to do your part as usual and wait for further instructions." The caller hung up.

These calls were a normal part of his day, and he

could have handled this any other day. Moms regularly overdosed and were on their death bed when he arrived to take the child. Usually the children were payment in exchange for the drugs that the addicted mom or even the dad took. Men wanted babies. The demand was high along with the risk. The job paid accordingly. But now Mike suddenly became sick and pulled the car over.

How could he continue after seeing what had happened to Sara? Yes, he'd seen it many times before, but now he was looking at it through new eyes—eyes of compassion and love. He stopped the car and opened the door, trying to get some air. After he took a few sips of water, he managed to compose himself. He started the car again and continued.

The phone rang again. This time, it was his new friend.

"Undercover officers have already raided the address that you gave us as the destination for the drop off for the baby. The occupants were arrested. When you arrive with the baby and mother, we can take them to a safe house where we have a nurse and medical staff to wean them both off the drugs. Boss Man will never know that his business is crumbling around him. He will never know the role you play. The plan is in place to start taking him down," the sergeant relayed before he hung up.

Mike was still thinking about the call when he pulled up to a deteriorating home that looked like it had seen better days. Paint was peeling off the siding; the porch was falling into the dirt. The baby cried inside the house. He looked around to see if he was being watched and then rushed into the residence. The living room was sparsely furnished with a couch and a dresser with a small TV on it. He walked into the bedroom to the left where the baby cried as she lay half-naked in the small dresser drawer on the floor. He was used to ignoring the bodies in the bed when he grabbed the children and was usually out of the house within moments. But this time, he took a moment to really look at the girl in the bed. Her body was so paper thin that he could almost see the bones. Ratty hair framed a face that seemed innocent despite everything she'd suffered. The girl couldn't have been more than seventeen. Anger stirred in him at the sight, and he held back tears once again.

On an impulse, he grabbed the girl with one arm and laid her over his left shoulder. With his free right arm, he picked up the baby. His own actions surprised him. As he left the dilapidated home, an angel held open the screen door to the living room.

He had no idea how he managed to situate both the mother and the child in the front seat of his vehicle. He looked at the baby carrier on the floor, and against his better judgment, placed her into it, setting it back on the floor out of sight. He prayed that he wouldn't be stopped as he drove as he had no idea how he would explain a baby in this unsafe position to police. He carefully buckled the mother's frail body in the seat as he pulled out the driveway.

A half hour later, he arrived at Paula's where she sat outside on the porch steps. He called her to come and help him.

Paula moved the carrier from the car into the house. She picked up the baby and held her, rocking her to quiet her down. Mike carried the girl into the house. He went to one of the bedrooms and laid her gently on the bed and found a blanket to cover her. Paula watched from the doorway as she held the baby. "Who is she? Who is this woman?"

Mike took a deep breath then let out a sob. "My sister."

———— ◆ ————

Senator Benson looked out of his office on the top floor. The view was the envy of everyone who graced his presence in the corner office. But today, it failed to calm him. He was the first one to arrive in the building every day and the last to leave each night. He took his government position seriously as he knew that the people depended on him. He often spoke on the hottest political issues of the day and had won the hearts of his constituents.

He turned around and sat down at his desk, opening his laptop to check his email before starting the day. His schedule showed three back-to-back appointments before lunch before he had to head to a speaking engagement at a nearby university with the business department.

He rose and walked over to his coffee pot, pouring another cup. Back at his desk, he reviewed several reports for his upcoming meetings.

He smiled as he read the first report, which showed the enthusiasm and the support he longed for in his community. The other two made little sense and looked as if they had been slapped together. He was a perfectionist and held high standards for those around him. His office manager excelled at her job and documented every email from constituents. No one would ever find so much as a single scrap of paper out of place in his office. He had covered his tracks well. His staff and organization kept his life and his office running like a well-oiled machine over the years.

He called for his driver to pick him up along with his interns. The drive to the university took ninety minutes, and he had business to attend to along the way.

———◆———

Tonya and Natalie enjoyed their lunch and roamed through the psychology department at the university. Natalie reviewed the catalog and circled the classes she wanted to take next fall.

As she turned the corner, she looked out a window that faced a parking lot. Some young men were taking a couple of small carrying cases from the trunk of a Cadillac. When an older man walked to the car to help them, she gasped. "Tonya!" she whispered.

"What is it?"

"That's Boss Man!" She pointed to the older man.

"You're kidding! No way! Don't you recognize him? That's Senator Benson. He comes up here to speak every few weeks. There is no way he's involved in what you've experienced."

"Oh, yes, he is! We need to call Sergeant Grant! Right now!" Natalie pulled out her phone and dialed the familiar number.

———— ♦ ————

"What do you want me to do, Mike?" Joshua asked. They were sitting in Wisdom's living room. Holly had brought over a tray of tea and cookies and set them on the coffee table. She sat in a chair across from Mike and Joshua and listened intently to Mike's request.

Mike's phone beeped continually with messages. He assumed that Sergeant Grant was desperate to reach him. "I need to take this call." He answered the phone. "Sergeant Grant, I thought it was you. You'll never believe what happened. I found my sister, Hannah. I recognized her because of a raspberry birthmark on the inside of her left ankle even after not seeing her for a decade. She is the mother of the baby I picked up. I brought them both straight to Paula's." Mike hung up his cell and looked back at Joshua.

"Seeing my sister lying on that bed of rags and listening to her baby cry broke my heart. It was way too much. I don't understand any of this. Why has all this happened?"

"Are we still discussing why you found your family like

you did if my Father is in control?" Joshua crossed his legs and leaned back. "I guess I could ask this: why weren't you there to protect her?"

Mike sighed. "You know why."

"Enlighten me."

Mike took a deep breath. "Seventeen years ago, my mother invited a man she was dating to move in with us. I was only ten and Hannah was just a baby. I thought that I would have a dad who would love me and take me to games and do things with me like my friends' dads do.

"Instead he turned my dad's shop into a dungeon for children. Worst of all, he imprisoned my mother and baby sister although he kept his activities a secret. They were not involved in any of it at that time. At seventeen, I found out what he had done. He took what my dad had once treasured and now used it to torture children. He then sent me off to live with so-called friends of his. I never saw my mom or sister again.

"He lied to all of us." Mike took a sip of his tea. Holly had placed a bottle of Anger Management drops next to his cup. He put some into his tea and smiled at Holly as she poured more tea in his cup.

Mike burst into tears. "I tried to save them, man, but I had no idea what I was doing myself. I was in a dungeon of my own. He groomed me to take over for him, but I didn't really understand that until it was too late. That day, when he drove me to the house, the man raped me. That was how he tried to make sure that I was stuck in this dirty business forever. To make matters worse, my stepfather then made me his partner. My job was to find children from drugged-out parents to sell to the same type of men as the one who raped me."

"Do you think that what you went through was your fault?" Joshua uncrossed his legs and leaned forward, resting his hand on Mike's knee in a gesture of bonding.

"I thought it was at first. He had my mother convinced that he was her knight in shining armor, taking her from a life of despair and debt left from my father's death. She worshiped the ground he walked on. There was no way I could tell her what he was doing."

"Who was in control?"

Mike thought for a minute. He knew it wasn't a trick question.

"You didn't want me to go through this. I know that. But why didn't you stop it?"

"I could have, and I wanted to. But the evil one caused this, not me. It was on his territory, by his hand.

"Like I stated before, it's a process. In some cases, I can just call ten thousand angels to go take care of a problem, but what's happening here is of such a large magnitude that it will take a while to restore. As a result, children have developed many issues, such as physical and mental developmental disorders.

"As I said, I could take care of this with one sweep of my hand, but I am restrained in many ways. This act is against my nature, and the battle is great.

"I need prayer warriors to rise up in this battle, but they have not done so yet. People must pull their heads out of the sand in order to win this battle. I am putting this burden on many hearts so that we can win this war." Tears formed in Joshua's eyes. "I hope they pick up their swords and start fighting soon."

Mike left Wisdom's home with more confidence and a better understanding of Joshua's point.

He reflected further on what Joshua had said about prayer warriors. He wondered who had prayed for him. He didn't know his grandparents on his dad's side as they lived in another state. Money was too tight to go see them. He hadn't seen his mother in years as his stepfather managed to sever that relationship.

He drove into the next town to Boss Man's new location. Night was falling, and he had spent a better part of the afternoon with his sister.

The day seemed like it had lasted a lifetime. Before he left, Mike made sure that his sister was safe. She was starting to show signs of life.

Marjorie, being a nurse at the local hospital secured needed items to help facilitate her recovery. She found additional help through the doctor and at Sergeant Grant's request. She was watching over his sister when he went to check on her.

But the baby had a sudden convulsion and then went into intense seizures. The withdrawal from all the drugs overwhelmed her tiny body. She fought to live, but in the end, the battle was too great. She died as Marjorie fought to save her tiny life.

Marjorie dreaded the moment when she would have to break the news about the baby to Hannah. She had put IVs in Hannah who was starting to gain some color in her pale skin.

Mike wished that law enforcement could just clean out the entire mess, leaving no reminders of what Hannah had endured. But he knew that doing so could cost them valuable evidence, along with the human lives they might put at risk.

"She was seven when I left."

"How did you know it was her?" Marjorie asked. She took a small sponge and placed it in a cup of water to wet Hannah's dry lips.

"She has a small raspberry mark on her left ankle. I saw it when she lying on the bed." Mike walked over to the head of the bed and knelt down, resting his head on his sister's chest, and cried. Hannah raised her left hand and caressed his hair. Her eyes were still closed, and she was breathing softly.

"We gave her medication to make her vomit the drugs she had in her stomach."

"Thank the medical staff for me. And tell Sergeant Grant I am sorry that I didn't follow the plan. I'm not sure if the Boss Man will know what went down or not. I have to go see him right away for my next assignment."

"How long is this going to go on, Mike?" Paula asked as she walked in the room.

"I wish I knew."

As Mike exited his car, he walked up to the main house on the property. He wondered how the Boss Man was able to secure places so quickly. The locations seemed abandoned and off the grid. At least this place felt as if it were more homey even if the girls that resided here couldn't truly enjoy it.

Upon entering the main house, he went to the parlor to the right of the front door. A desk and a few chairs were scattered throughout the room, and Mike made himself comfortable even though he feared that Boss Man would know what he had been up to in the last few hours.

A few minutes later, a car pulled up, and Boss Man got out and came inside the house, carrying a briefcase.

"Hey Mike! How did it go? The guys called and said the mom was a goner. The client just called to say thanks and let me know he transferred the money into the main business account. I have a check for your share."

Mike's jaw nearly dropped to the ground, but he managed to maintain his composure. He knew that the man was lying about everything, but he had no idea what Boss Man knew. He took the check handed to him.

"Up next, I've got two more for you." Boss Man took out two contracts. "Both of these girls are in way over their heads. Their kids are ours now. One is delivering at the hospital, and she listed you as the adoptive dad. We've already found a wet nurse for the baby, and the nursery is set up for the little one."

Mike looked—really looked—at Boss Man for the first time in almost seventeen years. He had grown older; his hair was graying. But when he was in the public eye, he presented a very different image to his constituents.

Mike wanted to scream at him. This was just a game to his stepfather.

He knew that Boss Man set Mike up so that Mike's own niece would be sexually tormented, just as he had done with so many others, but if you call it luck, the baby died before any man could touch her.

He wanted to jump across the desk and choke the life out of him for what he had done to his family. His lack of regard for his own stepdaughter and the way he casually stated that she was dead infuriated Mike. Where was his mother? Did she even know about any of this? Did Boss Man have a plan to comfort her during her grief or had she now become just as callous and evil as he was?

As the myriad of thoughts and emotions swirled through his head, he waited for Joshua to speak to him. He looked behind Boss Man to where Joshua stood. Joshua motioned for him to go find the girls. He would take care of the rest.

"Thanks, sir," Mike replied hoarsely as he rose to go to his car.

———◆———

Sergeant Grant hung up the phone after Natalie revealed who the Boss Man really was. He put his head in his hands, overwhelmed at the complexity of it all.

He had supported Senator Benson for years. How could he be involved? The question kept running through his mind. The man had an impeccable record with the voters. He was involved in many activities that benefited the welfare of children in the community. Natalie had to be mistaken. Why hadn't Mike told him about Boss Man's involvement earlier?

He picked up the phone and dialed a number.

"Mike, I've got a question for you. Who is the Boss Man?"

Sergeant Grant heard breathing on the line but no response. "Mike, are you there?"

"Yes. He's my stepdad, and he just set me up. He's had me trapped for years. I can't believe I'm saying this but, well, it's Senator Benson."

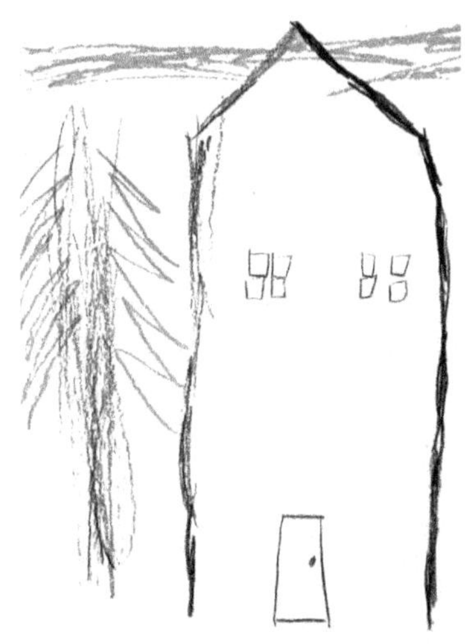

CHAPTER 9

Wisdom and Holly were sitting in their favorite spots on the front porch of The Father's Cabin, enjoying the quiet of the day. This entire case had drained them of all energy, and they both agreed that they needed a much-deserved break away from town and all the drama.

"Why do mortals have to tangle so many webs? Look how much they hurt everyone, even those who aren't directly involved," Wisdom commented. "No one wants to listen to logic."

"I agree. It's very hard not to go against their free will and pull them out of their messes even though they do it to themselves."

"Ladies," a male voice announced behind them.

"Joshua!" Holly exclaimed. "We had no idea you were here."

"I came home a bit ago. I'm just as concerned about all that's happening as you are. We need to bring Sergeant

Grant and Mike up here to spend some time if you could arrange it, Wisdom. Mike needs to sort out his emotions about everything that's happened with his family."

"His sister, Hannah, is holding on. But the baby didn't make it. Marjorie and Paula are doing a great job taking care of their guests. I would expect no less."

"Thank you for guiding Paula to open a safe house for these trafficked girls. Mike is bringing two more girls."

"Now if we can find an open door and a way to keep more children safe. The angels are doing their very best, but the enemy forces are still too strong. Once the prayer levels increase, the angels will have the necessary backing to accomplish their task."

"It is sad."

"People don't realize how much prayer works, especially when it's coupled with fasting."

———◆———

Hannah woke with a start. She glanced down at her left arm at the IV, trying to figure out where she was. She then studied her surroundings. She didn't recognize the room. This was much nicer than some of the rooms where she normally found herself.

She took a minute to realize that something was missing. The baby! Why wasn't she crying? Hannah screamed, and Marjorie rushed in.

"Where's my baby? What have you done with her?"

Marjorie took Hannah in her arms as the tears streamed down her cheeks. "I'm so very sorry, honey. She was such a little warrior. But she's resting now, safe in the arms of Joshua. I can only imagine how overwhelming all this is for you. Let me give some more medication to help you sleep. We can talk more soon."

———◆———

Two weeks later

"Good morning, sleepyhead." She turned her head to the right and felt a sharp pain in her neck.

"Ouch!" she exclaimed.

"Sweetie, let me give you some magnesium. It acts as a pain reliever. I can add that to the antibiotics and nutrients in the IV. Your body will be stiff for a while. You've suffered quite a trauma and have been in a coma for a couple of weeks."

"What! A couple of weeks? How is that possible?" Hannah watched as the woman left the room, only to return moments later with a syringe. "It's a low dose of magnesium. In this house, we believe in natural supplements for our patients whenever possible." The woman chuckled.

Hannah groaned. Her body had grown used to strong street drugs, and they helped her forget the dark circumstances of her life, especially now that her baby was gone. She needed those now, not some mild pain meds or a herbal remedy that might not even work.

"Where am I? And who are you?"

"Sweetie, I've told you all this before. You must have forgotten. You are safe now. Mike brought you here a couple of weeks ago. Those monsters left you for dead in that hellhole. He saved you. My name is Marjorie, and I'm an RN."

Hannah started to cry. "This wasn't how it was supposed to happen! I loved my baby so much and can't believe she's gone! And not only that, I am going to be in so much trouble! It would be better if I had died too!"

"Now, now, Hannah. I know you're upset. Why don't you try to sit up? I'll bring you something light to eat. Do you like fruit? Eggs? We will work everything out."

"Whatever you think is fine with me," Hannah replied. Her mind was elsewhere. How would she ever escape? This house belonged to the enemy. She knew better than to ever accept anything for free. Everything cost something. All she had ever known is that she gave others sex, and in return, they paid her with drugs.

Hannah looked at Marjorie in shock. "You said Mike brought me here. Who is Mike?"

Marjorie looked at the young girl. " He said he was your brother."

"I did have a brother named Mike. But he died years ago."

———◆———

Lydia Benson sat on her back porch, soaking up the sun for just a few moments. Her husband would be home soon, and she needed to check on the meal for the dinner party she was hosting that evening. She sighed, thinking about everything that she had done in the last week: luncheons, foundation meetings, planning committees—the pace never seemed to slow down. But enough reflecting for now; she needed to find some pep so that she could start preparations. Really, her life had been a whirlwind of one event after the next ever since her husband had become senator. While others saw the glamour of marriage to the popular Senator Edward Benson, the last seventeen years had brought untold heartache as well.

A couple of years after the wedding, they had moved to the mansion where they now live. The parties and social life became too much for her, so she tried to stay out of the limelight whenever possible. But the demands of her husband's job didn't make that easy.

Despite her dislike of Edward's government position, Lydia still smiled whenever she thought about how much he cared for her. They had lost a son ten years earlier in an auto accident as he drove home from school. Edward handled everything when Mike died, including keeping intruding reporters at bay. He had taken Lydia and Hannah to a beach house a friend owned until the media focus on the tragedy blew over.

Once she and Hannah returned home, they never spoke of Mike's death again. But still she grieved. She visited his grave every day at the local cemetery where Edward had a family plot. Once the funeral had passed, the town residents never brought up the matter either. Lydia wasn't sure if that helped her grief or made it worse. But she knew that Edward was trying to move forward in the only way he knew how.

Then Hannah disappeared six years later. She had a fight with Lydia the night she left. Edward wanted to take her with him to a constituent meeting so that she could learn about politics. He had future political plans for her. But Lydia had other ideas for her daughter that night. "I want you to stay home!" Lydia screamed at her daughter. Hannah jumped, afraid of her mom's overreaction. But clearly, there was much more to it than that. Hannah hadn't been her happy-go-lucky self ever since Mike had died. She was solemn and quiet and almost too obedient, especially considering how Mike had acted when he was the same age. Lydia lost the battle with Edward, and Hannah left with him.

When he came home that night without Hannah, he claimed that Hannah ran away. "I dropped her off at the door and then went to go park the car. When I went in the lobby area, she wasn't there. The clerk handed me this note." Edward took the note from his pocket, written in her handwriting.

"I can't take the grief and sadness in our household anymore, Mom. You just cannot seem to get past Mike's death. But you have forgotten about me and the pain that I am suffering. I am hurting too, and I can't watch you suffer any longer. I don't want to be a politician like Benson, either. I will come home after I have had some time to think.

Please remember that I love you no matter what. Hannah"

Lydia teared up at the memory even after all these months. She kept the note in her jewelry box. But none of it made sense to her. She had been gone for nearly a year. Lydia had not touched her daughter's room since Hannah had left in hopes that her daughter would walk back in the door any day. She looked inside but quickly closed the door at the rush of the memories. The maids never went in to clean. They had no reason to do so.

Lydia rose from her lounge chair and went into the kitchen to see how dinner was coming. The guests would arrive soon.

Edward entered the house through the garage door. He walked over to where Lydia stood at the sink, helping Holly prepare the hor d'ouevers, and took her hands into his own. He led her to the breakfast nook, and they sat down at the table. His back was to the window that looked out toward the hedge around the flower garden. Hannah had played there when they moved into the house years ago. The gardeners took a fancy to having a child around the grounds and fixed the area the way she liked. She shook her head in an effort to focus on brought her attention back to what her husband was saying.

"My investigators found Hannah in a flop house in the next county. She died of a drug overdose. According to the autopsy, she passed away forty-eight hours ago."

Lydia burst into tears. "No! Both of my children cannot be gone! I refuse to believe it!" She buried her head into her husband's chest and sobbed uncontrollably.

Edward asked Holly to contact the guests and ask them to come the following week for dinner. He helped guide Lydia up to her room where she stayed for several days.

———◆———

A week later

"Perhaps, sir, we should cancel the dinner," the cook observed as she watched Edward comfort his wife. "It's only been a week. Has she had enough time to heal?"

"No. The guests are just arriving." He glared at the cook and turned to hold Lydia's face in his hands. "Lydia, you need to control yourself through dinner. This is a very important dinner, and everything must be perfect." He looked at the cook. "Holly, please get my wife a cup of tea. But as soon as dinner is over, you need to immediately leave the premises. I will not have my staff making suggestions on how to run this household." Edward rose from the table and left to go upstairs to prepare for dinner.

———◆———

In a dark corner of a room, a young girl sat weeping. A door opened, the light from the hallway illuminating her tear-stained face. A man stormed up to her and grabbed the six year-old girl's wrist. Sara screamed out in pain. The man dropped her suddenly and stepped back, his mouth open in surprise. Sara looked beside her at the largest angel she had ever seen. He held a sword under the man's chin, and the man backed up. He turned and ran out of the room in terror. The angel was gone, leaving Sara to wonder what she had just seen.

A lady entered the room and told Sara to come with her immediately. Sara knew almost everyone who came and went from her room, but she had never seen this lady before. Still, she knew better than to argue. She rose and then dried her wet tears with her hands, wiping them on her pants. She knew better than disobey anyone's orders. She only hoped she could still go home.

CHAPTER 10

A year later

After a year of wading through tons of red tape, Natalie was finally starting her first class.

The first leg of what promised to be a long journey began after Natalie called Sergeant Grant before they left the university when she told him about seeing Senator Benson. Taking no chances, the lawman made arrangements for Natalie to go with the other officers. They arrived on the scene within minutes in an unmarked car and motioned for Tonya to go home. Tonya looked over her shoulder back at Natalie, hesitating for a moment. She turned and ran back to the other young woman, squeezing her in a tight embrace, tears streaming down both their cheeks. They knew they would never see each other again.

Natalie was then taken to another state where she was hired as a nanny for a couple with a young child. This couple had also suffered after their child was trafficked, and they had been relocated as well.

Natalie elbowed her way through the campus crowds, still trying to piece together all that had happened. How could Sergeant Grant have the opportunity to end this yet refuse to do so? She thought back over his words to her.

"This is a huge break in the case but brings us no closer to finding Sara. Anyone that has been involved in trafficking with Senator Benson—both the suppliers and the buyers—will still find other ways to continue their evil. If we tried to stop the operation now, Sara would just be sold to someone else. We want to find as many people as possible who are involved so that we can shut down the entire operation. We have a plan in the works, and it's coming along well. I know it's nearly impossible, but you have to trust me on this, Natalie. I am doing the best I can with the resources I have. I need another break, but I haven't found one yet."

With that, the sergeant closed that part of the case. A year later, they were still no closer to finding Sara despite their best efforts.

Natalie sat down at her desk in the classroom and looked around at the other students, most of who were about her age. She wore a sweatshirt and jeans and felt comfortable with the others as if she blended in. A couple of the female students were pregnant. Every time she looked at their swollen bellies, her heart stabbed in pain.

She opened her text book and pulled out a pad of paper to take notes. She looked around the room and saw that most of the students had laptops. She would ask Sergeant Grant for one. She had him wrapped around her finger, and she knew it. While she didn't take advantage of the situation, she did know how to make the most of it.

The class was surprisingly easy, and she began to relax. She loved taking human studies in high school. The workings of the human mind fascinated her, especially how it processed events. She could tell that some of the students had their own personal challenges as she did. But like her, they chose not to share what they had been through with the rest of the class. Several were from broken homes, and a couple of them had lost a parent during their childhood. She could relate to that. One had a child taken from the home by the courts because of her drug abuse. Natalie could tell that there was more—much more—to the story. The young woman's face seemed hard and cold. She made a mental note to speak with her someday if the opportunity ever came.

Her work as a nanny, thanks to Sergeant Grant, was bittersweet as well. The little girl reminded her of Sara, which was heartbreaking for her at first. She completely understood the suffering that the little girl's parents, Patsy and Dave, had endured although the circumstances were different. Their daughter had been taken from a shopping cart while the parents were distracted. The lady who took the child was talking with Patsy as if she knew her and was standing near the mother, the clerk later told the officer.

In a split second, the lady had grabbed the child from the cart and dashed out the door. Patsy and Dave dashed after her, calling for help, but another man blocked their way and tripped Patsy. She fell down. As bystanders moved to help her, the man disappeared in all the commotion but not before the girl's father wrote down the license plate number of the car the lady drove.

Several weeks later, the same lady was caught when she tried the scheme again at another store. The child was eventually returned to the couple, but they had to move and leave the life they once knew. Sergeant Grant put the family into witness protection for their own safety.

Soon class was over, and Natalie placed her book and notes inside her backpack. She didn't have any other classes for the rest of the day, and she rushed to catch the bus for a ride home.

Patsy was home getting herself ready for her nursing job at a local hospital when Natalie arrived. She kissed her daughter goodbye and waved at Natalie.

The precocious four-year-old, Emmy, was sitting at the table, coloring and chatting away with her imaginary friend. Natalie went to her room to quickly change into something cooler as the weather had warmed up. She returned to the kitchen to fix a snack for them.

"Mom said that she left half an apple in the fridge for me."

"Cool, kiddo." She peeled the apple and sliced it for Emmy with a little cottage cheese.

Dave arrived home a couple of hours later, threw his briefcase on the couch, and went into the bedroom to change into shorts, a T-shirt, and a pair of running shoes.

"I'm going for a run. I'll take Emmy with me. Is the running stroller in the garage?"

When Dave and Emmy left, Natalie made a cup of tea and sat down in the living room to study. She relaxed for the first time in a long time. After everything that had happened, she was finally beginning to feel safe also.

———◆———

Mike and Sergeant Grant were sitting at a bench by the Glass Sea. Joshua was walking on the sea and bent down.

"Mike, come here," he beckoned.

Mike rose from the bench and sat down on the glass. Joshua pulled up the earth with a swipe, and a dandelion appeared through the glass. Joshua picked it and handed it to Mike.

"A weed?" Mike asked.

"A flower. You can eat it; the roots provide nutrition, and you can use the flower to make wine or tea. Holly infuses the flower in water to make her essences. It has many uses."

"And you gave this to me because?"

"Your first thought was that I was giving you a weed. But I showed you the benefits of it. Sometimes we just toss out what we think is useless, such as the dandelion. If we don't learn from what we view as worthless, we won't see the beauty it actually holds."

"You mean how my stepfather sees a child in front of him when he gives me an order. He views that child as disposable even though that child is precious in the Father's sight."

"How did you feel the first time your stepfather sent you to pick up a child?"

Mike thought for a moment. "I was seventeen and still a child myself. I was terrified for the child because I knew what he would do to her. He threatened to tell my mother lies about me. Even though I did what he said, he still lied to her. I haven't heard from her since the day that happened." Mike looked at the dandelion. "I felt useless, just like this dandelion."

"How do you feel now?" Joshua asked. He lay down on his side on the Glass Sea, bending his arm and resting his head there. Grass grew up all around him. He was dressed in a green shirt and jeans. The wind began to blow softly, and his brown hair ruffled slightly in the breeze.

"I'm going back to my roots, just like this dandelion. I have begun to see my value again and that I am capable of bringing life back to the children, life that has been stolen over the years.

"Did you know that we have closed down several cell groups that were harboring children in compounds? We have also brought home several hundred children. Yet my stepfather doesn't have a clue that any of this is happening."

Joshua smiled. "Yes."

Mike laughed.

Joshua sat up. "Do you remember that every time Moses showed a miracle from my Father to Pharaoh, Pharaoh's heart was hardened? He is doing the same thing to your stepfather as you and Sergeant Grant take down his operation. His eyes are blinded so that he cannot even see what is in front of him. It will be soon, my friend. You are getting closer to Sara."

"I can't thank you enough for what you have done in Hannah's life. She is alive and well. The ladies enjoy her company so much."

"It's a beautiful sight to see," Joshua replied. He motioned for Sergeant Grant to join them. "Now we go into a new plan of action, a new strategy of attack." Joshua sat up and began to push back the earth and manipulate it in order to make his point. He pulled up a continent. "We need to go here. It will cause an earthquake in the Boss Man's operation."

"He is involved here as well?" Mike's eyes widened.

"He has spread his net of evil far and wide, much more than anyone can fathom. No one is safe here. Let's get to work."

———◆———

Paula surveyed her surroundings. Christine and Sara had now been missing for four years. She knew that Ray was doing his best. But she knew why his best wasn't good enough in her eyes. They were her children, and they belonged at home. Her eyes again welled up with tears as she reflected on all she was missing in their lives. She wondered if they were even alive.

She looked around her circular driveway and at the rose bush that the Boss Man's minion had trampled the day the girls were taken. Despite the beating it had taken, it had survived what should have been a fateful demise. She smiled. The reminder of her husband's kindness and how he knew what brought her joy blessed her. On the day he found out he had cancer, he planted the bright floribunda that had bloomed large flowers each year since his death. Even a bully's big feet and cruel aggressions could not destroy it. In a way, she felt that maybe the hardy flower represented her daughter and granddaughter; despite the attacks against them, they would still survive.

Hannah had found a job at a boutique in town and loved it. She was finishing her education at home and would graduate this year. Paula and Marjorie taught her and the other girls that lived with them. Paula was very proud of her and hoped she would contact her family to come to the celebration they were planning. Neither Hannah nor Mike had mentioned her one word about her family since she had arrived.

Now that she thought about it, Paula hadn't seen Mike around since Hannah had arrived. It took several months before Hannah was able to trust anyone and that included Mike once she understood what had happened. For brother and sister their relationship was somewhat strained, but Paula could see that Hannah was beginning to forgive Mike for not saving her. Paula shook her head and went into the kitchen where Marjorie was making sandwiches from the homemade bread she made earlier.. Paula enjoyed her company and was glad that Marjorie had moved in. Together they had grieved and rejoiced over the years. The quiet companionship helped them form a strong bond.

As true prayer warriors, they prayed together daily. With the help of Holly and Wisdom, they worked togeth-er to help the girls that Mike brought to the house that he saved from further trafficking. The final goal was to get them safely home to their loved ones. After every sting operation, law enforcement officers brought the girls to

Paula's house, which had been transformed into a halfway house. The girls were bathed and cared for and nurtured back to health, both physically and emotionally.

Trust was the biggest issue with the girls. At first, they struggled to even believe that Paula and Marjorie wanted to help them. In fact, they considered them enemies. The only life that the girls had ever known was being taken to meet a john who would pay for sex. Once he finished using them, they were always on the road, on their way to the next one.

Paula and Marjorie patiently worked with girls but without much success. The girls had built up such walls that everyone was an enemy to them, including the two women who had given so sacrificially.

Hannah, on the other hand, was a gem and an answer to their prayers. She took the young girls under her wing and spent time building their trust. The trafficked children understood each other intuitively. It didn't take long for them to begin to trust Hannah. That trust soon transferred over to Paula and Marjorie. The children sometimes stayed there for weeks before being reunited with their families. Paula's home was a safe sanctuary where they could begin to heal.

Paula worried about all the hours that Mike and Ray were investing into the case as they worked tirelessly to break the trafficking ring. But they were no closer to finding Sara. Ray told Paula what had happened at the Glass Sea. She knew that their goal was to find Christine and Sara, but as she looked at the girls who were now living in her home, she sighed in despair at the magnitude of the great task before her. She wondered if the men felt the same way: consumed at the enormity of it all.

Mike called to check on Hannah and make sure she was doing well. Paula didn't know the circumstances with the congressman, so she had asked Mike if she should call his parents. Mike's response scared her. He told her that none of them could contact his folks. His parents had kicked them out, and that was all she needed to know for now.

At Paula's home, the phone rang. It was Hannah. "Can you come pick me up? I missed the bus."

"Certainly. I'll be there in a few minutes," Paula replied. She hung up and went straight to the boutique.

Upon arriving, she glimpsed a former neighbor, but she couldn't quite place her. As she parked and exited the car, she waved, but the lady didn't see her. Paula retrieved her purse from the vehicle as thoughts of the tragedy her friend had endured swirled through her mind. Seventeen years ago, she had lost her husband in an auto accident that left her and her children devastated. He had no life insurance, so the family was nearly penniless as well. In addition, she had a mountain of debt and two children to feed.

Once in the store, she looked again at her friend. Recognition clicked in. This woman was Mike and Hannah's mother, and Paula's former neighbor, Lydia.

Before Paula could talk to her former neighbor, Hannah called out to Paula that she was ready to go. Paula looked back and saw Hannah standing next to her car. She looked back and forth between the two women before finally returning to the car. "I'm starving. Do you mind stopping right now to get a burger? My treat." Hannah replied as she got into the front seat after the doors were unlocked.

Puzzled, Paula just looked at Hannah. "Sure, honey. That would be great." She kept her voice calm as the reality of the situation dawned on her. Her temperature rose along with her frustration. She went to the driver's side of the car.

Her mind was racing with questions as to what Hannah was doing in the middle of this situation. Did not her mother know what was happening? Why didn't she fight for her daughter? And what about Mike? How was he involved? Questions flooded her mind, and she had no answers. But she didn't spend much time focusing on the questions. She couldn't explain why, but she just sensed that she needed to get Hannah out of there quickly.

"Paula? Are you okay?" Hannah asked.

Paula looked at Hannah and smiled. Hannah had obviously not seen her mother in the store. "I'm fine, sweetie. Burgers would be wonderful."

Once Paula and Hannah returned home, they decided to rest.

Paula needed a cup of coffee even though she knew it would make her more jittery than ever. Still, she filled the coffee maker with water and a scoop of coffee grounds. While she waited for the coffee to brew, she stepped out her kitchen door to Wisdom's cottage. Wisdom was on the front porch watering her potted plants in the window box.

"Do you have a minute?" Paula asked when she reached the steps.

"I've got all the time you need, honey," Wisdom replied. "I just made some tea. Would you like some?"

"Yes, please." She was so distracted that she forgot about the coffee brewing in the kitchen.

Paula followed Wisdom into her cottage. As Wisdom poured the tea into two cups, Paula smiled. She had been concerned about her water and electric bills increasing now that she had a guest house in her back yard. But the bills had been supernaturally taken care of, so she dismissed the thought. She noticed that even her own personal bills had dropped down to nearly nothing during the last couple of years. She had been blessed by Wisdom, Holly, and the others who had stayed and watched over her.

"What's troubling you?" Wisdom asked.

Paula looked down in her lap. "I'm really puzzled."

"About?"

"Why a mother would abandon her children. How could someone do that? Look at what we've seen walk through our front door during the last couple of years. Girls not even old enough to drive are having babies because being pregnant is a fantasy and a thrill to some perverts. Then the babies are sold like cattle at an auction." Tears formed in Paula's eyes, and Wisdom handed her a tissue.

"I know Hannah and Mike's mother. We were friends years ago, but when she remarried that rich man, she had no time for us so-called little folks anymore. I know that she doted on her children when she lived across the street from us. She never let them out of sight for a moment after her first husband's death. I wonder what changed.

"I thought Hannah saw her today at the dress shop, yet the girl didn't even react." Paula sat back in the chair. "The day Sara was taken, Lydia was over at the house across the street. I saw her when I ran out of the house, and I was getting ready to call out for help when her—" Paula stopped for a moment. "—her husband! Oh, my word! It was him!" She stood up. "He was here! He was the one who was ordering me around! You saw him! You had to know who he was!"

Wisdom quietly leaned back in her chair. "You needed to figure it out for yourself, Paula."

"That man! No, he's less than a man! No real man would treat people, let alone girls and babies, like that! And to think I voted for him!" Paula was seething as she back down. "How did I not recognize him before?"

"You were under quite a bit of stress," Wisdom replied. "Sometimes our minds can temporarily block out people and events."

"I need to let Ray know." Paula started to rise. But just as quickly, she sat back down. "He already knows if Mike told him." She looked over at the back of her house from the porch. The scent of lavender trailing alongside the cobblestone path from the kitchen door to Wisdom's porch slightly calmed her. "What those children have suffered! If he is capable of taking my daughter and grandchild, I can't imagine what Mike and Hannah have gone through!" She looked at Wisdom, her tone deadly serious. "This has to stop. Now!"

The extreme heat wore out the girls. The house was hotter inside than it was outside. They wanted to rest, but Madame had said no. They were to entertain the men by the pool. Madame promised to turn the air conditioners on when they were each in the appointed rooms with their johns.

Sara was used to the routine as she had been made to obey orders many times during the last few years. She glanced around the room, measuring how long the others had been there by the expressions on each girl's face. The eyes of the newer girls filled with tears as they did their best to put on a brave front. Those who had been there for a few months grumbled under their breaths, their frustration and anger showing. But those like her who had been there the longest seemed to resign themselves to the inevitable. Sighing, Sara put on her string bikini and a white cover up.

Sara tried not to stare at the girl sitting across from her while she had her make up done. But she couldn't help but see the bruise forming on her cheek or the bulge of her belly when she leaned forward. The oversized T-shirt hid the pregnancy well.

Sara said nothing, but she knew what would happen to the girl once the Madame found out that Maggie, her closest friend at the brothel, was pregnant. If a girl suspected that she was pregnant, she would first go buy a pregnancy test. The girls knew that they needed to hide the pregnancy for as long as possible. But Madame now required every girl from the age of nine on up to take a monthly pregnancy test. Some men preferred pregnant girls, so they were secluded in their own section for a time. Sara didn't know where they went, but she saw the girls and the negative shift in their attitudes when they came back to Madame's house. They were mean, angry, and despondent for a long time afterwards. Some of them refused to go back to work when they returned, so they were beaten to force them to comply.

"I'll make the room ready for you," Maggie stated as she cleared off the makeup table.

Sara took the pony tail out of her blond hair and brushed it out. The men wanted young girls for the sex but, at the same time, didn't want them looking like little girls. When it came to their appearance, they had to walk a fine line to balance between the two.

As Sara stepped out the French doors of the pool house, a man in the pool called out to her. She robotically untied her cover up and jumped in the pool, splashing and laughing with the man that was old enough to be her father. She knew how to act out the role she had been forced to play. But her vacant stare betrayed the emptiness in her heart.

Sara woke up in the dark room and couldn't even see her hand in front of her face. She was groggy from the drugs they usually gave her. As usual, she grabbed the sheet from the bed to cover her naked body as she went to the bathroom to clean up as she felt unusually sticky. But this time, the sheet wouldn't budge. She blinked again to try and clear her vision. She knew that someone was lying next to her, but the john was usually gone by the time she woke up. Five years of this life had stolen her innocence, and she was used to the routine. She reached over to touch the person next to her but felt an icy cold body. A scream escaped her young lips.

Madame rushed in and turned on the light. Sara gasped at the baseball bat that Madame grasped in her hands. Then they both looked in horror at the mess on the bed. The sticky stuff on the sheets was the man's blood; she was covered in it.

Madame grabbed Sara and rushed her out of the room. She banged on a door, and Maggie opened it. Madame glanced down at the other girl's exposed stomach and groaned. "I'll deal with you later. For now, take Sara and get her cleaned up. Then hide her and the other young girls down in the basement. When you finish, come right back up. I need you to be the girl that the police find here, not this one." Madame pointed at a blood-covered Sara. "I have to call the police. Now."

Sara couldn't decide which was worse: being stuck in these situations or constantly moving. When would she ever find her way back home?

———◆———

Sergeant Grant wanted to punch a wall. The harder he worked on the investigation, the worse that it seemed to stall. Yet he knew the man behind it all. His frustration increased at the thought. Paula now knew everything and had told Sergeant Grant about Lydia. But worst of all, her friend was married to the jerk. He needed to find a way to infiltrate the organization and tear it down from the inside until all of it landed on Congressman Benson. But for now, the politician had his hand in too many community groups and activities. His constituents would be appalled if they knew about all the illegal activity that he was involved in as well.

Sergeant Grant had sensed that something was off with the congressman's wife. Sergeant Grant had heard rumors about what the congressman said about Lydia's daughter. They said that she had passed away, but he knew the truth about her. Even so, he had to keep quiet about it as the cover up of her death was considered part of the on-going investigation. The lawman was well aware of Congressman Benson's manipulative tactics, and he knew that Lydia was deceived as well.

Sergeant Grant sat down at his desk and reviewed all the elements of the case once again. Then he smiled as an idea formed in his mind. He called Paula. "How would you and Wisdom like to take Lydia to lunch today? My treat."

———◆———

"Good morning, graduate." Natalie opened her eyes to see Dave and Patsy at the door with a breakfast tray laden with her favorites: French toast, scrambled eggs with cheese, extra bacon, and a side of salsa.

Emmy ran in between them and jumped up on the bed. "I helped!" She giggled as she crawled into bed next to Natalie.

Dave placed the tray down on the bed in front of her. He and Pasty sat down on the small couch across from her bed. As she devoured the delicious meal, the three of them chatted.

"So what are your plans now?" Dave asked.

"I'm not sure. I have submitted apps to mental health clinics and counseling services, but nothing has opened up yet. I'm beginning to think that my clinical work at the drug rehabilitation center was in vain."

Dave looked at Patsy, and the two of them grinned. "What?"

"I have a small office at the clinic. It's not much, but it's a start. You can have it as your own office. I have a second room that you can use for therapy."

"Seriously?"

"Seriously," Dave said. "When you are done eating, we'll go take a look."

Natalie loved her new office and the therapy room. Within a month, word got out about Natalie's work with children from various streams of life. She began building her clientele.

After a few months, she looked up to see a familiar face in the clinic: the student she had met the first day of classes. Her name was Amy, and she had brought her little girl. Natalie uncovered numerous details from Amy's story. She was able to help put the little girl's abuser behind bars in a matter of weeks.

———◆———

Mike called the police sergeant.

"What's up, buddy?" Sergeant Grant asked.

"Care to fill me in on what's been happening?" Mike asked. "I understand that your girlfriend and my mom have been meeting for lunch lately. How did this come about?"

The lawman took a deep breath. "Do you remember anything from your childhood when your dad was alive? Do you have any memories of where you lived?"

"Not really. I was only nine when Mom and Edward married. By the time I was a teen, we had moved to the mansion. That dirtball had given me so many drugs that I could barely remember my own name."

Mike sat back in the driver's seat of his car. After this was all over, he was going to burn the vehicle. Too many horrible memories were associated with it that he wanted to forget. But he still had a reputation to keep.

"You should talk to Paula," Sergeant Grant replied. "Leave me to find the kids that the congressman is playing mind games with." He paused. "I might not be in her life after today after she hears what I have to say."

"Why, what's up, buddy?" Mike asked sarcastically. He was in a mood and communicated that now to the lawman.

"I am bringing Christine home. She wants to join us in taking this scumbag politician, your so-called stepdad, down. I think she's ready."

Mike sat up, accidentally hitting the car's alarm button. He scrambled to shut it off as he asked, "And what about Paula? How do you think she will feel about the fact that you've hidden her daughter away from her for all this time? And why are you just now bringing her back?"

"Mike, it's for the best. The last family that I placed Christine with was murdered in cold blood. She and their little girl escaped and contacted me. I thought she should come home."
"If you think it's best, go for it."

"It's time to go see Joshua again. We'll certainly need his help."

"Are you afraid of your girlfriend?" Mike laughed.

"No, of course not. I'm worried about Christine." Sergeant Grant ignored Mike's sarcasm. "I didn't want to leave her where we found her years ago just to have her fall back into the same trap. If you saw her now, you would be amazed. She is not the same young woman you saw at the compound who was just on the brink of death."

———•◆•———

Natalie was now calling herself Christine again. She was finally sitting in one of many cars on a passenger train in the middle of the night. Emmy was asleep with her head in her lap. After the execution of her father at his office and the attempt on their lives, she suffered from PTSD. But Christine hoped they were safe now. The car was dark, and they had it to themselves. They were finally going home.

CHAPTER 11

"I swear, Ray! If I wasn't so madly in love with you, I'd kick you out of my house and out of my life! But knowing you as I do and with everything we've been through in the last five years, I just can't do that. As crazy as our relationship has been, I know you had good reason for what you did, so let's hear it! I'm all ears!" Paula stood up from the couch and walked away from Ray to get some space. She looked angrily back at him and, for a moment, almost felt sorry for how she was acting despite her legitimate reasons. Ray's hair was thinner and grayer now, accentuating the bags under his eyes. She thought about all they had gone through during their relationship and the love that they had shared. All of that was now at a critical moment. She was no longer sure that she could trust this man she loved.

"So you are aware of all Congressman Benson's done over the years," her boyfriend stated. "About four years ago, he had a compound outside of town, an old camp area with cabins and a rec room and a meeting hall with a kitchen and showers. One day, he and his cronies up and left the compound with the other girls. But he left Christine there alone in one of the cabins.

"When we found her, she had been there alone for at least three days. She was dehydrated and so thin that we didn't even know if she would survive. We put her in hiding with a couple who worked with girls in trafficking, and they nursed her back to health.
"It's been a tough road for her, but she has fought to recover. You would be so proud of the young lady she is now."

"And you hid her to protect her from that scumbag congressman?" Paula asked, her brown eyes blazing. Tears sprung to the surface, and he thought about wiping them away. She didn't deserve this pain. No one did, but she was one of the sweetest people he had ever met.

"Yes. We had no idea why Congressman Benson left her for dead, and we didn't want him to know she was still alive."

"And Sara?"

"We have some strong leads." Ray said. "Oh, and one more thing. Christine is bringing a seven-year-old girl with her."

"I have another grandchild?" Paula whispered. This time, the tears really began to flow, and Ray stopped resisting his urge to comfort her. Rising from the couch, he wiped them away with his fingers as he took her in his arms.

"No. She was a nanny for another couple for the last four years. That child was almost sold into trafficking too, but we found her before the transaction took place. We put the family in protection. Christine was at work with the little girl, Emmy, when she heard the gun shots in Emmy's father's office. She hid Emmy in a cupboard, and Christine crawled under a desk. The shooter left the building as quickly as he entered, never checking the room where they were hiding.

"Christine drove home with Emmy and saw the police already at the house. She knew that Patsy was dead, so Christine went to the train station with Emmy and then called me.

"I already knew about the murders and was trying to locate Christine when she called. She had Emmy with her. If I moved her to another location, I either had to remove Emmy or send the child with her. But the best choice was just to bring her home with Emmy. The little one will be safe here."

"Who are these people that are so cruel?"

"People I never want you to meet," Ray replied. "We can't take Emmy to any of her family members as they are targets too. Emmy is the property of the traffickers in their minds, and they will do everything you could imagine—and more—to get her back.

"I'm sure that you, Holly, and Wisdom would love to have her company and input. She has great news to share with you," Ray replied as he stepped back from Paula.

"Where is she?" Paula asked, drying her eyes.

"Right here, Mom."

Paula gasped as she looked at her daughter who stood there at the front door, holding the hand of a scared little girl. She was no longer the thin bony young girl of many years before who was passed out on the couch.

A professionally dressed woman in a dark blue pant-suit now stood before her.

Paula sobbed as her prodigal daughter walked into her arms. They held each other for a very long time, and the two wept together. When Paula finally let go, she looked down at the young girl standing next to her daughter. The child mirrored Sara's features: the depth of her nose, the cupid bow's lips, the upturned nose. It was almost as if Sara were home again.

"Welcome, Emmy. I'm so glad you are here." She looked up at Christine who was still wiping tears from her eyes. "Words can't describe how happy I am to see you again. And you're so healthy!"

"Yes, I am. And thank you, Mom. I never thought I'd be happy to be home again. I wondered if I'd ever come back. I know your prayers kept me safe all this time."

CHAPTER 12

Lydia finished making her bed and straightening up the room before the maid came in to clean. She still had to organize before cooks and maids came even though she'd been living the dream of having household servants for the past ten years.

Her husband had either been campaigning or in office since the day they met. Edward had given her anything she wanted during their marriage, which she deeply appreciated. But all the money and material possessions in the world couldn't stop her grief at the loss of her children.

Tears formed in her eyes as she thought about the fact that she would never see them on earth again. Drug abuse had taken the lives of both her children, and even after all this time, she didn't know how she would heal. Her husband had graciously put their ashes into decorative urns for her, and these were now on the mantle over the fireplace in their bedroom. She planned to eventually take them to the sea and bury them with their father. But so far, she had not felt up to the task.

Her cell phone rang, and the caller ID lit up with Paula, her old friend and neighbor. She was so grateful for the restored friendship they again shared. Many times after her husband's death, Paula had come and spent the night with her, helping to ready the children for school the next day. Paula treated the children as if they were her own, watching them and spending time with them until Lydia met Edward. They met for coffee many mornings after she sent them off to school as Lydia stayed home while Benson worked. In return, Paula's children stayed with Lydia and the congressman from time to time overnight while Paula and Brad went out.

She decided to wait and call her back later. She let the call go to voicemail.

Lydia went downstairs for a snack. Holly, her favorite cook, was still in the kitchen. Her husband had threatened to fire her a couple of years ago, but Lydia managed to persuade him to let her stay.

Holly had a plate of fruit and cheese ready for Lydia when she came downstairs along with a carafe of her special blend coffee. The coffee helped strengthen Lydia emotionally. Despite her happiness in her marriage, she still struggled with the challenges life had handed her.

Holly poured herself a cup of coffee as well and sat down at the table with Lydia. Over the last couple of years, they had developed a much more intimate relationship than employer and employee. Lydia encouraged the relationship as she truly enjoyed Holly's company. She made Lydia feel safe, which she hadn't felt in a long time.

Despite the financial security that Edward provided, Lydia had felt off-kilter for the last several months. She couldn't put her finger on what was bothering her, but the nagging feeling wouldn't go away.

"Is your snack okay?" Holly asked, noticing Lydia's puzzled look.

"Perfect, thank you." Lydia replied. She stared out the window, her blue eyes vacant. "The wisteria is blooming nicely, making a beautiful backdrop to the rose bushes and the heather, don't you think?"

"I agree. I have an herb garden at home as well as several flower beds. I make my essences from them. It's so peaceful walking around Doubters' Hollow."

"A name like that doesn't sound very peaceful." Lydia cringed.

"It's all about perception, Lydia. Sometimes what you hear or see at first isn't what is truly real".

"I wish I could believe that." Lydia sighed. "Paula said almost the exact same words the other day at lunch. She lost her daughter to drugs as well. How do you find the beauty in that for your children?"

"Your children and Paula's daughter used the drugs to bury their pain.

"Unfortunately, a bad habit will only provide a brief respite from the pain. But you as a parent can determine how you will handle it. You can create a life for yourself. It's up to them whether they accept the boundaries that you set."

Lydia nodded her head in agreement and sighed. "It's too late for me now. But I still want to help Paula. Why don't we take her lunch to surprise her?"

Holly sat back and smiled. Already plans were in motion to make this transaction as safe as possible. Paula's home would continue to be a refuge. "I'll put together lunch while you get ready. You can take the lunch over to her. I'll stay here and start dinner."

———◆———

Joshua was sitting by the Glass Sea when Sergeant

Grant arrived. "Hey, man! How's it going?" Joshua asked him. The lawman had always been taken back by Joshua's lack of formality.

He never got used to it even though Joshua treated everyone the same way. Some of that had to do with his own upbringing in such a strict church. But Joshua had never felt that he belonged in that house of worship. Ray had to admit that he could more easily relate to Joshua's informal style of conversation.

"I'm getting better, thanks. As you know, I pulled Christine back in. That might have been against my better judgment, but I think it was time. Too many fires are brewing close to home, and I'm afraid I will miss something. If I would have left her out there for any longer, she would have been in trouble. By the time I realized it, it would have been too late to help her. Better to bring her in now before any mistakes were made."

"Let me show you something." Joshua got up and walked on the Glass Sea. He bent down and drew on the glass. As he sketched, the image of Paula's home appeared. White orbs surrounded it, and two large angels with big swords stood in front of the driveway. Ray could see the tiny outline of Wisdom's cottage in the back.

"You are seeing from our perspective now. Remember when we were in the room with Sara? This is how it always looks."

"Amazing! I knew that Paula's house was a sanctuary."

"It is. Christine will be safe there with Emmy."

"Thank you, Joshua." Ray turned around. His jaw dropped at the unexpected sight of Christine standing there.

"I know that look. You think I don't belong here, that I don't know about Joshua and this place. What about Mike? Did you treat him the same way?"

Ray was taken aback at her words. He couldn't get used to the transformation in the young woman before him. He still remembered her as skin and bones with yellow teeth and greasy dark hair. Her threadbare clothes had barely covered her, and she reeked of sweat due to the lack of cool air in the dark cabin and the infrequent showers. The fear in her blue eyes had told him the most that day of the rescue. But now, her blue eyes blazed with confidence in stark contrast to how she had looked then.

"Ummm, that's not exactly what I meant. I guess I'm surprised to see you. And you look well."

Christine was still not sure about this man and his intentions. "I met Holly that morning when you found me. She set up a beautiful table for me, and I ate to my heart's content. She loved me in a way I hadn't known in a long time. I have every right to be here," Christine continued. "Were you like this when Mike first came to meet Joshua? Mom told me about the court case and how Mike is now a confidential informant. Why would Joshua treat me any differently?"

"It's not the same. Mike committed numerous crimes and should be serving time. But he reached a plea agreement with us, so he is working for us now. You have already served your time."

"But I sold my daughter for drugs. Do you think I that I deserve to be here?"

"That's not for me to judge," Ray answered.

"But you can judge Mike."

"It's the law, Christine. Why are you so concerned about him?" the lawman asked. The two of them had forgotten about Joshua who was still standing on the lake, listening to the entire conversation. Sergeant Grant softened his tone. He didn't like the direction that this conversation was headed. He already knew the answer to his question.

"I asked Mike to join us as we need to plan a strategy

as we move forward." Joshua broke in. "Sara is in a lot of trouble right now. She desperately needs me, but she has forgotten who I am. This often happens to children when they are stolen. They suffer so much abuse. As with all children, I am still there for her, but she can't see me anymore."

Sergeant Grant and Christine did not realize that Mike had arrived. He was sitting down on the lake with Joshua. "We have a lot to cover in a short time. We had best get started."

Two hours later, Sergeant Grant was back in his office, inputting notes into a secret file that he kept on his personal computer about the case.

Crash! Bang! He jumped up and ran to the main lobby to check out the source of the noise. A few minutes later, Senator Benson came into the lobby to pay Mike's bail. Sergeant Grant watched from the hallway, his heart breaking. He wished he could just arrest the congressman on the spot with all the evidence he had in his file, yet he still had nothing concrete. If they intervened now, they would never find Sara.

CHAPTER 13

Paula and Lydia sat on Paula's front porch. Paula could see that the fresh air, the smell of the nearby roses, and various herbs that Paula planted around the porch was helping to bring a color back into Lydia's face that hadn't been seen for some time. She was looking well again. So much so that Paula was concerned about deceiving her friend, yet the little voice in her head told her that it was okay. She knew this was part of the plan.

The pain still shown through Lydia's eyes, and Paula knew she held the answers that her friend longed for.

Paula smiled at the typical signature that Holly had left on the lunch. She would never have believed it if anyone had told her that living a kingdom lifestyle would include all of the following: angels guarding her property, Wisdom residing in her back yard, and the Comforter of all comforters living in the spare bedroom of the home she owned and fed her and the occupants in the house so lavishly.

Paula's only worry in the past five years was getting her family back. Everything else had been taken care of for her.

"Paula, have you heard any more about your granddaughter?" Lydia asked. She poured a cup of coffee from the carafe that Holly had packed in their lunch. As usual, Holly had left nothing undone for this lunch. She had put fruit salad in separate bowls. The aroma from her freshly baked bread wafted through the air.

"Nothing. It's as if she vanished into thin air. If it weren't for my friends, I don't know what I would do."

"I know just what you mean. I don't know what I would have done without Holly. She has been such a life-saver to me. I had no idea how weak I had become mentally or physically. When my first husband Ryan died suddenly, I had to step up and try to make some sort of a life for my children. You and your husband were such a blessing to me during that difficult time. When I got the job at the courthouse as an administrative assistant, I had no idea how my life would turn out" Lydia looked at her friend. "Have I ever told you how Edward and I met?"

Paula looked at Lydia. That time had been a whirlwind, that much Paula knew. "No, you hadn't from what I recall anyway. I'd love to hear it." Paula thought about what she had just said. She would actually. How did a man like Edward think about her friend? Did he really love her at one time? Love was not a word Paula could equate with a man like Edward..

"One day, I was sitting out in my car during lunch, and I just started bawling from exhaustion and the weight of all my responsibilities. Edward was a lawyer then and was always at the courthouse. He saw me and offered to take me to lunch. He literally swept me off my feet and took care of all our debt. The kids loved him. I used to get so angry because they spent more time with him than me.

"Right after we moved into the mansion, I became very sick. Edward hired a nurse to take care of me. I rarely saw my children during those first few years as I was bed-ridden. I had nearly forgotten all of this until now.

"Then one day, my son was gone. Edward told me he had been in an automobile wreck and didn't survive. I wanted to see the body, but he convinced me that I wasn't even well enough to leave the house. I'm not sure why I accepted what he said. I was just so tired from not feeling well. Still, I should have fought harder. This was my only son!

"But I comforted myself with the fact that I still had Hannah. She was a brilliant student. Always brought home straight "A"s. Last year, Edward told me she had died of a drug overdose." Lydia started to cry and looked across the yard at her former home, now a rental. Lydia loved this quiet neighborhood and the neighbors who helped keep her afloat even when she didn't notice. She looked over at Paula. "Why would my husband lie to me about so many things? Why did he lie about my children when he knew how much they meant to me?"

———◆———

Joshua sat on the front step, looking out over Doubters' Hollow. That was not the name that he had chosen for it. It was Holly's garden and where she went to think and plan. She loved the name and felt at home once the name change was complete.

Holly loved the dark places. She felt most at home in those spots, and her garden seemed to flourish in its new atmosphere. Joshua was amazed at how she took to Doubters' Hollow like a fish to water.

He rose to go for a walk to the village. When someone from earth came up to the mobile courtrooms, the villages were abuzz as they knew a family member had temporary access to the heavenlies.   It wasn't uncommon to see residents of heaven lurking around when court was in sessions

As he walked in the village, he spotted one of the women whose home was in one of the local villages standing at the back window of the chancellor's home. The chancellor was entertaining and signing scrolls for a guest. Joshua walked up behind her, gently placing his hand on her shoulder. She turned and fell into his arms weeping. Her soft brown hair was damp from an earlier shower. The skirt of her yellow dress puffed up in the breeze.

"Oh, my child!" Joshua whispered in her ear. "Weep tears of joy as your husband is happy. . But remember, he has never stopped loving you." Joshua released her and took her face in his hands. "It won't be long, and he will be here permanently. For now, you can only see him from a distance. Grab the stroller with the babies, and we'll walk to the courtyard in the village. We can watch from there as he interacts with the angels. The chancellor will join you for lunch and fill you in on what's happening." Joshua took one hand and grabbed the baby stroller with the two newborns who had never breathed the air from earth. Together, they left the chancellor's home.

———— ♦ ————

"Gee, thanks for bailing me out, 'dad,'" Mike sneered at Senator Benson. "Whoever ratted me out has another thing coming!"

"You think I did this?" Congressman Benson asked. The two of them were at a secret location. Mike wondered how many similar places his stepfather had access to over the years. In his years as senator, he had managed to acquire a number of properties through drug raids. Mike figured that the politician had set these up himself. Mike didn't know exactly how powerful the man was nor how much he had his hands in the proverbial cookie jar, but over the years that his stepfather had held him in captivity, he had learned more than he ever wanted to know.

"Cat got your tongue, Mike?" his stepdad sneered.

"What?"

"I've got a job for you. Are you going to take it?"

"Not today. Call me tomorrow. I'm beat."

"Suit yourself. I needed you to move some inventory from one of my businesses to another location. They are rather new pieces, so I didn't want them damaged. I know you will take extra good care of them." His stepdad handed him a slip of paper. "Here's the information with their current location and the delivery address. Report back to me when you're done. And take the van." He tossed his stepson the keys.

———◆———

Wisdom traveled back to her beach home in heaven for the day. She had several homes located throughout the kingdom. She loved the sound of the sea; it calmed her and helped her think, giving her great insight into her problems. She invited Holly to join her. Their plan was to help calm down Lydia before she met Edward again.

Wisdom went to the kitchen to make some tea while Holly waited in the living room. They were expecting Joshua any moment.

The three of them had worked well together since the beginning of time. Wisdom was even personally described in the Book. The people written about in the Book back then were really no different than people today. They struggled with life's circumstances and faced the same physical and emotional difficulties.

"I'll be in there in a minute, Holly. The tea is nearly ready."

"Okay. I am making a special blend for Lydia to help

calm her as she will soon find out all that has happened over the years."

"Can I have a boxing glove to punch out the adversary?" Wisdom asked as she poured tea into the cups on a tray. She laughed to show that she was joking, but Holly knew that she was angry at the devastation he had caused. She found cookies in the freezer that Holly had stored a few weeks ago.

"Ladies, am I welcome to join this party?" Joshua asked as he opened the screen door.

"Is there anywhere you are not welcome, Joshua?" Wisdom greeted him with a smile.

"Several, actually. Including some churches. Remember The Father's Cabin?" Joshua replied as he took a seat on the couch. He crossed his legs and leaned back on the arm rest.

"And that is why we all get along so well," Holly responded.

"What ideas do you have to help Lydia?" Joshua asked.

"I am making sure that the medications that her husband has been giving her will not cause permanent damage or affect her too drastically. He is very deceptive."

Joshua sat quietly as the two women discussed how to comfort Lydia. Wisdom finally noticed that Joshua was deep in thought.

"I know that look," Wisdom said as she picked up a cookie from the plate. She sat down on the floor with her legs crossed. The sea air was reaching deep into her soul, and she relished in it.

"And you, my dear, are in your element," Joshua replied as he sat up. "Remember when Jacob's sons told him that Joseph had died? He mourned for years."

"Lydia is living this out now as she thinks that her very own Joseph—Mike—is dead!" Holly exclaimed.

"What are you thinking, Holly?"

"That it's long past time for Mike and his mother to meet."

"Mike isn't ready yet. He and Hannah both believe that she kicked them out," Wisdom replied. "When Joseph knew who his brothers were, he hid something valuable in one of their bags."

"What valuable does Mike have? What would cause a reaction from Lydia?"

"Mike has Sara now.."

"And Lydia has access to where Sara is, but she doesn't know it yet," Joshua replied. He looked through the floorboards of Wisdom's home to the earth at the scene below. Holly and Wisdom both gasped. "There's nothing we can do now." Holly replied.

"No, evil again has won for a time," Wisdom observed. Joshua wept.

Mike drove the van through the dark night into an alley. As he pulled up, he looked over at the six girls waiting in the shadows. They ranged in age from eight to fourteen. The older girls calmed the younger ones, and a couple of them had on large coats to keep them warm in the cold night. They huddled together, attempting to protect each other.

As Mike exited the van, his breath blew a puff of white mist in the cold air. He walked around to the other side of the van to open the door for the girls. They were cold and scared, but Mike had plans securely in place to make sure that they were done with this life in trafficking before they even reached their destination. Paula was already making up cots at home to provide them with a place to stay, and Sergeant Grant had men acting as lookouts, ready to raid the building once the girls were safe.

As each girl climbed into the van and took a seat, his heart broke as the light showed the despair in their eyes, the same darkness and the death that he had seen in so many others ever since he had switched sides.

The last girl, who was about ten, started climbing into the van but struggled and stumbled because of the over-sized coat that fell to her ankles. She was the smallest of the bunch. Mike leaned back to pick her up, and she turned her head, staring him full in the face.

It was Sara. She looked up at him, her eyes widening and her jaw dropping as the words stuck in her throat.

At the solid hit to his head from behind, Mike fell and blacked out.

When he came to, his head was pounding. He tried to focus on his surroundings. He shook his head from side to side a few times, hoping to clear his thoughts. Dawn was breaking. As he sat up, he stared at the open door from the back of the house where the girls had come from earlier in the dead of night.

The congressman's feet thudded down the rickety back steps as he approached Mike. "Thought you could double cross me, huh, son?"

"You knew that Sara was here the whole time."

"I did. And I knew that once you found her, you would go to great lengths to protect her. What a great show to have your buddies knock you out. But now, I need to know." He paused for effect. "Where are my girls?"

"Your men knocked me out and took them." Mike said as he got up.

"My men are inside."

"I don't have them! And now, I don't have my daughter either." Mike glared at him. "Tell me, why does it bring you such joy to destroy my family?"

"Edward!" The heavyset man turned around to face the direction of the voice. The shot rang out in the early morning, and Edward's heavy body hit the ground.

Mike looked in shock straight at the small frail woman walking toward him.

"Mother!"

"It's okay, son; it's over now. I know everything. Go find your daughter."

"Mother, do you realize what you just did?" Mike asked, taking the gun away from her and setting it down.

Within moments, several police cars swarmed onto the scene. Sergeant Grant exited his squad car. "We were waiting for your call to raid the house, Mike. When we heard the shots, we rushed right over. What are you doing here? Where are the girls?" The lawman looked down at the politician's body and swore. "We're going to need another plan."

The other officers were reading Lydia her rights and handcuffing her. Mike watched as his mother was led away. He yearned to help her with every fiber of his being. He looked at the sergeant, his eyes pleading.

"I'll do what I can to help her," Sergeant Grant replied as he furtively looked over his shoulder. None of the officers were watching him as he led Mike back to the van. "Go get yourself checked out and get to Paula's. I'll call you later."

"Ray, Sara was one of the girls. I saw her! I picked her up as she was struggling with her coat . . . . "

"What, Mike? What are you talking about?" Sergeant Grant stammered. Just then, the coroner pulled up behind the van.

Mike looked over at the congressman's lifeless body and then back at his mother. "He is still manipulating my family. My baby is having a baby. And in some twisted way, I will probably never see this baby again. The liability is too great."

The sergeant helped Mike to the van. As Mike

slammed the door shut, he looked at the lawman, the fear evident in his eyes.

"The girls. They're gone. They are no longer on Congressman Benson's payroll. Someone else took them. What will happen to them now?"

Author's Note

If you don't think trafficking's a big deal and if you don't believe it affects your community, this article and the following statistics might help you change your mind. Trafficking is a huge problem locally, nationally, and globally, and here's why.

Traffickers trap children and adults into the trade through lies, threats, violence, financial bondage, and other methods. U.S. federal law calls this a crime if the victim is younger than eighteen years of age.

Methods of trapping victims vary drastically and can include false promises of acting, dancing, modeling, or other types of so-called work. Other victims are manipulated through romantic promises and then forced into prostitution. Family members might sell children into the sex trade. The trafficking situation can last days, months or even years.

Victims can be nearly anyone: American citizens, foreigners, men, women, or children. Vulnerable populations, such as LGBTQ individuals and homeless teens, are often targeted. Sometimes victims work as escorts or in fake massage parlors, at truck stops or in brothels.

Trafficking jumps exponentially around the location and timing of national special events: the Super Bowl, the Olympics, and other occasions. The influx of people and the demand for those in the sex trade leads to an increase in victims.

Polaris oversees the operation of the National Human Trafficking Hotline, a 24-hour toll-free service with operators who speak more than two hundred languages. The Department of Health and Human Services established the NHTH in 2007[1]. It is funded through private donations.

The National Human Trafficking Hotline has reported 22,191 sex trafficking incidents inside the country since 2007. About one in six runaways (children younger than eighteen) are probably sex trafficking victims, according to a 2016 report from the National Center for Missing & Exploited Children.[2]

The NHTH received 8,759 reports of human trafficking in 2017, which included more than 5,000 traffickers and more than 10,000 victims.[3] The number of cases increased 13 percent compared with 2016, with an estimated 80 percent of victims identified as women and girls.[4] Ethnicity was only reported about one-third of the time, so specific numbers are not known.

The industries that are most-often named in reported cases of sex trafficking involve escort services, residential services, and outdoor solicitation. Victims report they are recruited via marriage and partner proposals, familial rela-

---

1   Staff, Human Trafficking Statistics 2017, "Human Trafficking Search," Accessed June 13, 2018, http://humantraffickingsearch.org/human-trafficking-statistics-2017.
2   Ibid.
3   Ibid.
4   Ibid.

tions, and those who pose as benefactors.

California, Texas, and Florida respectively have received the most reported cases of any state. Officials believe this is due to their proximity to the border, high immigrant populations, and the overall number of people. These states use all available resources to battle trafficking as well.[5]

The following statistics on human trafficking come from the website www.dosomething.org:

A slave costs an average of $90 around the world.[6]

Human slavery includes prostitution, the creation of pornography, and involuntary servitude.

An estimated 80 percent of trafficking includes sexual acts.[7]

Teens that enter the sex trade in this country average in age from twelve to fourteen. Many of these were sexually abused as children and ran away to escape their tough upbringing.

Illegal drug trafficking, arms trafficking, and human trafficking are the top three international crime industries in the world. Human trafficking generates a reported profit of $32 billion annually.[8]

The U.S. State Department lists many ways that you can combat sex trafficking. You can also become involved at a grass roots level and pay attention to anything that possibly looks out of place around you.

---

5   Ibid.

6   11 Facts about Human Trafficking , "Do Something," Accessed June 13. 2018, https://www.dosomething.org/us/facts/11-facts-about-human-trafficking.

7   Ibid.

8   Ibid.

ABOUT THE AUTHOR

Cheryl lives in the Pacific Northwest with her husband. They have one adult daughter. Cheryl loves to read, write, sew, knit, homestead and bead. Her life work is blessing the elderly and the less fortunate as she instills hope into their lives beyond their own limitations. She oversees a prayer and healing ministry. She is also passionate about the cause of human trafficking and protecting the most vulnerable members of society.